AFRICAN WRITERS SERIES

Editorial Adviser · Chinua Achebe

2

BURNING GRASS

AWS

This series makes available a wide range of African writing: both original works and reprints of already well-known books are included. Orange covers denote fiction (F), blue covers non-fiction (NF), and green covers poetry (P) and drama (D).

1	*Things Fall Apart*	CHINUA ACHEBE	F
2	*Burning Grass*	CYPRIAN EKWENSI	F
3	*No Longer at Ease*	CHINUA ACHEBE	F
4	*Zambia Shall be Free*	KENNETH KAUNDA	NF
5	*People of the City*	CYPRIAN EKWENSI	F
6	*Mine Boy*	PETER ABRAHAMS	F
7	*Weep not, child*	JAMES NGUGI	F
8	*A Book of African Verse*	*edited by* JOHN REED *and* CLIVE WAKE	P
9	*Modern African Prose*	*edited by* RICHARD RIVE	F
10	*Equiano's Travels*	*edited by* PAUL EDWARDS	NF
11	*One Man, One Matchet*	T. M. ALUKO	F
12	*The African*	WILLIAM CONTON	F
13	*Mission to Kala*	MONGO BETI	F
14	*Quartet*	*edited by* RICHARD RIVE	F
15	*Origin East Africa*	*edited by* DAVID COOK	F
16	*Arrow of God*	CHINUA ACHEBE	F
17	*The River Between*	JAMES NGUGI	F
18	*The Imprisonment of Obatala and other plays*	OBOTUNDE IJIMERE	D
19	*Lokotown and other stories*	CYPRIAN EKWENSI	F
20	*Child of Two Worlds*	MUGO GATHERU	NF
21	*The Only Son*	JOHN MUNONYE	F
22	*The Second Round*	LENRIE PETERS	F
23	*The Origin of Life and Death*	*edited by* ULLI BEIER	F
24	*No Easy Task*	AUBREY KACHINGWE	F
25	*The Concubine*	ELECHI AMADI	F

Fulani herdsman

Cyprian Ekwensi

BURNING GRASS

A story of the Fulani of Northern Nigeria

Illustrations by A. Folarin

HEINEMANN

LONDON IBADAN NAIROBI

Heinemann Educational Books Ltd
48 Charles Street, London W.1
PMB 5205, Ibadan · POB 25080, Nairobi
MELBOURNE TORONTO AUCKLAND
SINGAPORE HONG KONG

First published 1962
Reprinted 1963 (three times),
Reprinted 1964 (twice), 1966

Printed in Great Britain
by Butler & Tanner Ltd, Frome and London

for Michael Crowder

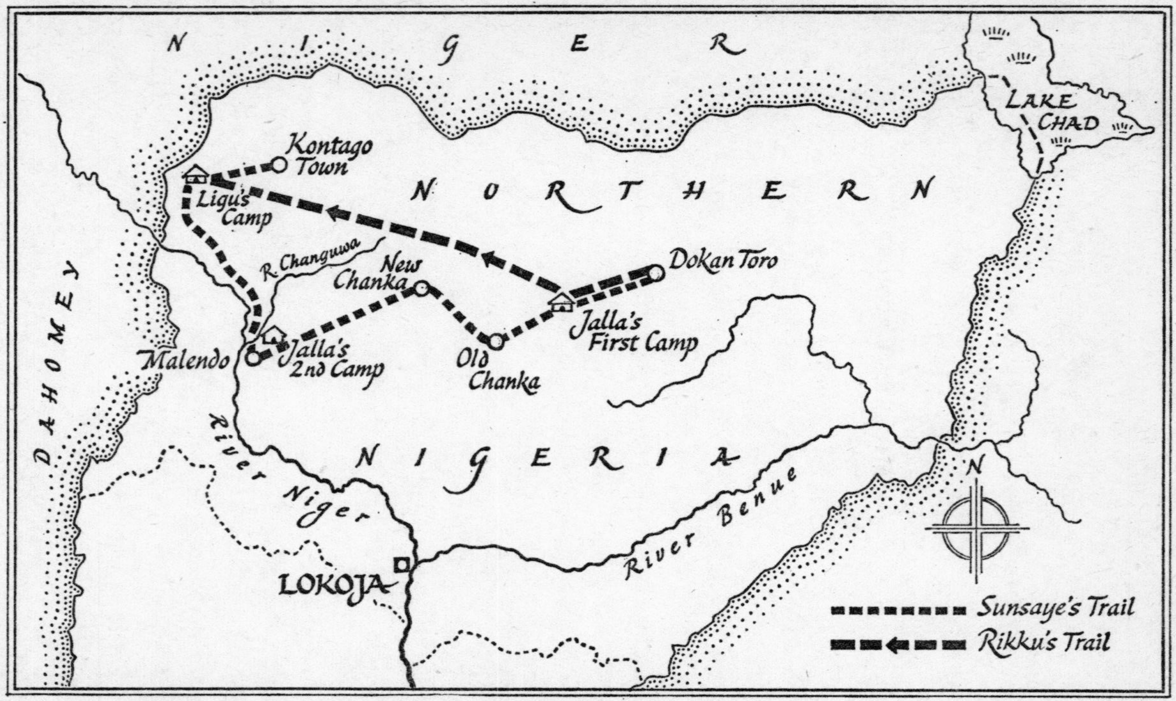

Sunsaye's journey

CHAPTER ONE

When they begin to burn the grass in Northern Nigeria, it is time for the herdsmen to be moving the cattle southwards to the banks of the great river. And the hunters, lurking on the edge of the flames with dane gun, bow and arrow, sniff the fumes and train their eyes to catch the faintest flicker of beasts hastening from their hiding places.

It is time too for the harmattan to blow dust into eyes and teeth, to wrinkle the skin: the harmattan that leaves in its wake from Libya to Lagos a shroud of fog that veils the walls and trees like muslin on a sheikh.

* * *

The old man sat still, tolling his chaplet. The trees were skeletons bleached in the sun—barren, with peeling skins bruised by decades of thirst and hunger. He sat with his son in the dry atmosphere of Northern Nigeria and on the grass beside him lay his bow and quiverful of arrows steeped in poison. The somnolence in the air crackled. Gusts of heat rose from the earth and shimmered upwards to an intense blue sky that hurt the eyes. He could smell the smoke fumes and he knew they were burning the grass. He and his son lifted their eyes and took in the undulating hills, the rivulets and rocks. And it was lonely. But they were nomads, wandering cattlemen, and loneliness was their drink. So they rested under the dorowa tree not talking, the son leaning on a stick the way fowls stand on one leg on a thirsty day.

When the girl came running towards them they saw the terror in her eyes. Close on her heels came a dark-visaged man, frowning and cursing, brandishing a *koboko*. He stopped when he saw the girl throw herself against the old man's feet and cry out to be saved.

"She is my slave!" he roared. "I want her back! She's running away!" He raised the whip.

"Your slave?" said the old man, leaping to his feet. His son's glance met the girl's, caught the mute appeal.

"Your slave," the old man said, "you're not fit to wipe the dust from her feet; yet you call her your slave. Listen! I'll make you an offer, you ruffian!" He turned towards the boy and said, "Rikku, can you find your brother Hodio?"

"He's down by the stream," Rikku said, "with the cattle."

"Go call him, by Allah!" He took out an arrow from the quiver and fixed it. "Yes, go call your brother Hodio."

"Hodio!" Rikku shouted. "Hodio! . . ." He disappeared down the hill. His father looked squarely at the burly stranger. "She's your slave?"

"I should have said, my master's."

"Has your master no name?"

"Shehu."

"The killer?" said Mai Sunsaye. He had heard of a man called Shehu who was said to be a swash-buckling ex-soldier discharged from the Cameroons campaign of 1914–1918. Shehu, the story went, lived to fight. He lived to cause confusion. Like an elephant, once offended he never forgot and never forgave, so the storytellers said. It would be unsafe to anger him.

Sunsaye turned when the twigs crackled behind him. Rikku and Hodio, arguing lustily, ran towards him. Hodio was senior to Rikku by five years. At nineteen he was tall and loose-limbed; athletic as a leopard, narrow of hip and wide of shoulder. The Sunsaye family acknowledged him as the man of tireless energy.

"Hodio, I shall ask you something," Sunsaye said.

Hodio knelt down reverently before his father, then rose and stood alert. "I am listening, father," he said.

"You see that girl?"

Hodio looked down at the figure sprawled before his father. She was ragged and the cloth draped around her body under the arms was torn, but Hodio noted the animal eagerness in her eyes. She had a rare face. Most of the Fulani girls were light of skin with straight noses and thin lips like those of the white people; but Fatimeh seemed to be a cross between Fulani and white. Her nose was tip-tilted with large nostrils, her hair was thick and black, though matted with dirt. She had red lips. She could not be more than eighteen.

"I have seen her," Hodio said.

"What d'you think she's worth?"

"Worth, father?"

"Yes, Hodio. This man, here, claims her for his slave. I cannot let such filth tamper with so lovely a maiden. I want to make him an offer."

Hodio moved nearer his father.

"You want to bring her into the family?"

"If Allah agrees," Sunsaye said.

Rikku watched Hodio, and he felt the girl's eyes fixed even more appealingly on his face as though he and not Hodio had the deciding word in her future.

"Five cattle," Hodio said, and turned to face Rikku. Sunsaye lowered his bow.

"That is much," he said. "Among our people a man may marry a maiden for two or three head of cattle. But he shall have the five cattle as you say. Drive them up." He stroked his beard. "The girl is ours. You may keep the cattle. Thanks be to Allah." He struck his breast.

"I warn you," cried Shehu's servant. "As long as you keep Fatimeh with you, you shall have no respite! Shehu will pursue you and kill you one by one. He never forgives!"

Mai Sunsaye laughed. He turned to the girl and said, "Rise!"

She seemed to have lost some of her terror now. She rose, but immediately flung herself down on hands and knees and called Allah! and prayed that Sunsaye might live for ever. The old man smiled and patted her head.

Together they watched Shehu's servant drive the five cattle up the hill until the thorns hid him from sight.

"Allah be merciful," Hodio said.

"Amin!" answered Sunsaye and Hodio in chorus.

Mai Sunsaye stroked his beard. "If he is really the servant of Shehu, then they're in luck."

"How, father?"

"They have beef enough for one year." He smiled. "But with her!" And he indicated the girl, "They have trouble enough for ten years!" He patted her on the shoulder. "I trust you will not bring us too much bloodshed. You heard what they said about Shehu. He will rest after he has torn you away from us. Ha!" He was talking in an undertone, as though to himself.

"Come," he said, raising his voice. "Let us be getting home. Rikku's mother will have some food waiting for us. You'll wash and wear some of her cloth, and rub oil on your skin."

It was always "Rikku's mother". She was his only wife, though under Muslim law he could have had three others beside her. He loved his wife, but the centre of his life was his love for the boy Rikku, his youngest son.

Sunsaye led the way along the dusty path, and Rikku and Hodio stood aside. "Hodio, go, drive home the cattle."

"Rikku. Come, let's go." Hodio was always jealous of the preferential way Rikku was treated. He spoke aloud so his father might hear. He had also said that one day he would do something to hurt father and son, to wound both deeply. "Let's go! Or are you hiding under our father's shadow? Allow Fatimeh to get home first, then admire her. Come!"

His father smiled. "Ah-ah! . . . Rikku, mind him not. Go along, now."

Rikku sighed and ran down the slope to join Hodio who

was already kicking up his heels and waving his herding sticks as he ran towards the valley where the cattle grazed.

Far away in the open fields on the horizon the grass was still burning.

CHAPTER TWO

The girl was silent enough. She learnt a lot and quickly. In one month she could milk the cows, separate butter and cheese from the milk, ferment the milk and cook nearly as well as Rikku's mother. At first she went with Rikku's mother to hawk the sour milk, but she was beginning now to find her way to and from town.

Hodio was enamoured of her elegance from the first. She must have known this because whenever he was sitting alone in the fields, dreaming of her, she would darken the grass with her shadow and he would turn and see her.

"I'm going to sell milk," she would tease, shaking the loops of her copper ear-rings in the manner of a coquette.

"Oh! But is this the way to the town? Where's my mother? Aren't you going with her?"

"She's still at home. I only came here to see you first." She would smile and the large gourd would sway while she bent and tilted her neck—oh, so gracefully!—to regain her balance. She was always chewing tobacco flower, so that her lips, teeth and gums were always red. Hodio noticed that her looks had improved since she came to live with them. Her skin was tight with new flesh, and it shone.

"Goodbye, Hodio! I'll be back in the evening!"

Towards nightfall when Fatimeh came home she often took a pot and went down to the stream where she bathed and drew water. Sometimes Leibe went with her, sometimes Shaitu, but she was never alone. One evening when the grassland was cool and he could hear his own flat feet against the dusty road, Hodio stalked her down to the river and told her to make ready to run away with him because he loved her and wanted her to be his wife, but Fatimeh's refusal was quite definite. She must have known that as a slave girl she could never hope to marry a free-blooded and proud Fulani like Hodio Sunsaye. Hodio knew that, too, but he waved aside her objections.

That evening the family sat around the big fire, telling folk stories, husking tomorrow's millet to the rhythm of folk tunes. Old Sunsaye was reading his Koran near the hut and listening with half an ear to the family conversation. All that Hodio did was to fix his eyes on Fatimeh's face, watching her for a sign which never came. Yet whenever he was alone she would come to him and when she went to market she bought him presents. One morning as he rested under the dorowa tree, she came again. She was on her way to market, she said, making eyes at him. Hodio spoke to her again. They would run away and live in a town where no one cared about tradition and custom. He would find work and she would mind the home. Fatimeh agreed to consider more deeply what he had proposed. He watched her swaying down the slope. She stopped by the stream to wave at him.

* * *

Old Sunsaye it was who first missed Fatimeh. He called Shaitu. And Shaitu said, "I haven't seen her." He asked Rikku, and Leibe, and no one could tell him where Hodio and Fatimeh were. They looked at the back of the hut and the horse was no longer tethered there.

Sunsaye followed the tracks of the hoof-marks to the stream and out across the scrub. "They're gone," he said at last. "Hodio has run away with Fatimeh." He pronounced the words with fear, as if he had always feared that this running away would mark the beginning of the rift in the family.

Soon he found that Rikku sulked. While Fatimeh had lived in the camp with them, he had noticed that Rikku had been happy. But now Rikku began to talk of Fatimeh's beautiful face and graceful manner, her clear voice beside the fire spinning Kanuri folk tales or singing. Mai Sunsaye knew it was mere calf-love which would soon pass. "If Fatimeh were here . . ." was all he heard from morning till night.

Rikku's mother was exasperated. "Fatimeh, Fatimeh, Fatimeh . . . every day, Fatimeh! You will not let us hear anything else!"

"There now, Shaitu," Mai Sunsaye interposed, "the boy admires Fatimeh so much! Let him alone; surely admiration is no crime?"

"I—I do not love her," Rikku protested.

"So!" his mother sneered, "you do not love her; yet you leave your meals untouched. You are careless with the milking of the cows; you wander about at night sleepless! Cursed be the day when your father bought that slave!"

Sunsaye called the boy one evening and spoke to him with deep concern. "My son," he said, "you are suffering. You have made an idol of this young Fatimeh . . . but come, sit down; let us talk."

Rikku sat very close to him, watching the dancing firelight in his beard. "It is the way of the world, my son," said Sunsaye. "Let me speak to you as a man, though you are so young. If you lose one girl take up with another."

"She loves me," Rikku said. "She told me so."

"It is no good, Rikku. She loves you, but she runs away with your brother."

Rikku raised his voice. "Hodio forced his will on her; her heart is still with me."

The old man gazed reflectively into the fire. "Do not be anxious, Rikku; everything will come right."

"I am ill. I—I do not think I can go to the grazing fields tomorrow."

"And Hodio gone! The cattle will all perish, by Allah!"

"I cannot go, father! In Allah's name!"

"*Wal-lahi*, my sons mean to break me in my old age."

Rikku rose abruptly. In a week he had become so ill that Mai Sunsaye was frankly anxious. Nothing seemed to do any good. The cattle were suffering. To hire a herdsman would be expensive. No one would ever induce an outsider to work as a son would. Plainly he had to do something definite, and soon too.

He took a decoction of roots and herbs to Rikku and sat beside him, watching him make faces at the bowl. He placed his long sensitive hands on the boy's neck. It was warm and throbbing.

"Rikku," he said, tenderly. "What do you want me to do?"

"Bring me Fatimeh," the boy said. "I want her back with us."

He laughed. "Are you in your senses? Were you not here when she ran away with Hodio?"

Rikku's eyes looked hurt. His feverish lips trembled. "You are the Chief of Dokan Toro. Your word is law, father. You can find them."

"That is true," said the old man. "In Allah's name, it is true."

"If only we can bring her back," Rikku said.

Mai Sunsaye sneered at him. "There'll be trouble. Trouble enough; for Hodio will always be at war with you. Brother against brother. O abomination! In our own family! Broken is the family; gone is the pride of the Fulani."

"Make an effort, father! I want her back but . . ."

Mai Sunsaye's eyes locked with his. "I shall consider it, my son." He spoke with energy.

"By the help of Allah, if Fatimeh is still breathing in this world of ours, I'll find her and bring her to you."

"I'm very glad, father. May your life lengthen."

Miraculously, Rikku's health began to improve.

CHAPTER THREE

Mai Sunsaye sat outside the hut, reading under the dorowa tree. He was much versed in the Koran, and he read and wrote Arabic with a fluency not unusual among high priests of the wandering Fulani. He made charms and amulets, he doctored the sick, he was a sage highly respected in the village of Dokan Toro. From far and near, his clients brought him their wounds of body and of soul.

As he pored over his books his neck ached. He was an old man, but he seldom spared himself or even remembered that tiredness came easily these days. He lifted his head so as to ease the muscles of his neck. It was a simple act, such as a man might unconsciously perform a hundred times a day. But for Mai Sunsaye, it was a decisive act.

In that particular interval of time, his eyes fell on a dove. It was nothing, really, just a Senegal dove, grey-breasted and red-toed against the sun-dried leaves. Mai Sunsaye saw hundreds of Senegal doves every day because he lived in their natural habitat, the sparsely wooded thorn scrub. That day he had seen, oh, he had never really tried to count them. They were always there; mating, eating the grain, cooing in the woody patches that dotted the endless veld.

"*Kuku-roo-ku-doo! . . . kuku-roo-ku-doo! . . .*"

He tiptoed across the clearing among the dung, with the fowls scattering to left and right of him. The dove had seen him. It had stopped cooing. It looked suspiciously down, golden eyes rolling. A quick flutter and it began to climb from branch to branch, skipping lightly. A talisman—a small rectangular white fold of parchment—was clearly visible to Sunsaye. It trailed after the dove as it skipped.

With his weak eyes he followed the bird's movements, straining hard against the glare of the sun. And then he saw it leap out of the tree and flash away, sweeping over the shimmering grassland and describing huge exciting arcs. He was barely able to see it drop into a tree. His robe caught against the thorn scrub, and every now and again he paused to adjust the sandals and to ease his feet.

If only Mai Sunsaye had at that moment remembered the *sokugo*, that charm of the Fulani cattlemen; a magic that turned studious men into wanderers, that led husbands to desert their wives, Chiefs their people and sane men their reason, Sunsaye would have refused to pursue the dove any further. Instead, all he could feel now was an exhilaration of the spirit that gave a strange buoyancy to his whole bearing. He felt he could easily grow wings and overtake the dove.

The dove had alighted in a low gardenia with twisted branches. He fixed his eyes on that tree, and as he approached he heard it cooing again. He broke through the thorn thicket, scurrying the bush rats, frightening the duiker into the blazing sun. He cursed as a black mass uncoiled itself and slid swiftly under the grass. A cobra!

"*Kuku-roo-ku-doo! . . .*" came the sweet, enticing notes. He saw the flutter of wings, the climbing out of the tree in little hops, until, at the topmost branch, the dove took off. He swore. He shaded his eyes and admired the graceful agility of the dove. The bird swept big arcs in the sky, made sudden deceptive dives as though intending to alight, spread its tail fanwise to act as a brake; and suddenly it froze and seemed to drop into a date palm. Sunsaye knew a short cut to that date palm. *Turn back now!* He seemed to hear the words from somewhere inside him.

But he went forward, not stopping to question, and followed the dove with the talisman as it lured him on and on; farther and farther into the grassland and the thorn trees and acacia gum. On he went till the sun sank lower and lower and dipped below the horizon and dusk came, and he was hungry and thirsty.

In the thorn forest, in the very heart of rock and stream, darkness could mean encounter with the agents of swift death: the big wild cows, the leopard. But Mai Sunsaye was beyond caring.

* * *

Mai Sunsaye's wife, Shaitu, had been out to sell sour milk in the neighbouring town. When she stooped to enter the next little hut where Mai Sunsaye often sat, her copper ear-rings dangled. She did not let it cross her mind that he

But he went forward, not stopping to question

could be anywhere else but within the settlement or that if he was not he would be far away.

Her daughter Leibe lay sleeping on a mat. She shook her. Leibe awoke and told a story of three strange men she had seen that afternoon. She said that the men came with a cage full of birds and let out one dove with a talisman attached to its foot. She led her mother to the back of the hut and showed her where Mai Sunsaye had been reading. Flung about in some haste was a book, a slate, an over-turned ink-pot—all Mai Sunsaye's.

Shaitu looked about her for a clue.

"There were three men," Leibe said. "One was a Chief."

"How d'you know?"

"Mother, he wore a crest on his turban."

"They must be evil men. I suspect it is your father's rival Ardo and his people. Since the people chose your father as Chief, Ardo has never been happy. He has sought to do away with him by malicious gossip. And now he has brought on him the *sokugo*."

Shaitu's life, like that of any other cattle Fulani, was ruled by beliefs for which she could find no logical explanation. She accepted happenings but associated them with inanimate objects and peculiar circumstances. A talisman could bring luck . . . A man may strike his enemy down by calling his name aloud and firing a needle into the sky. A man could send his enemy wandering to his death by striking him with the *sokugo*, the wandering charm. This was what she concluded had been done to her husband. Her belief in omens and portents was steadfast, and Leibe's description tallied with the manner of the black magicians among the cattle Fulani. Liebe told how Ardo men let out a dove with a talisman tied to its foot, how the dove flew into a tree with Sunsaye following after it. She was only a little girl and Shaitu hearing the details she gave knew she was telling what she had seen.

"They have struck him," she concluded. "It is the *sokugo.*"

It could only be the *sokugo*, the wandering disease. Now she knew he would wander after anything on the wing, until someone destroyed Ardo's magic. Thus did the *sokugo* deprive men of their stable lives and send them stupidly wandering.

How to punish Ardo? When Rikku returned from the grazing fields they must think of a way.

* * *

Shaitu waited and waited. It seemed to her that Rikku would never come home. At last she saw him in the valley among the cattle, lumbering slowly towards the camp. She did not return his smile, but helped him tie up the cattle for the night and light the big smudge-fire that kept away the leopards and the hyenas. When they had finished, Rikku asked casually, "Where's father?"

"I haven't seen him," Shaitu said carelessly. "But I don't think he's gone far!"

"He seldom goes out!"

"I don't know, Rikku. I returned and did not meet

him." She gave him a bowl of gruel. "Drink this, my son, and don't worry. You must be tired after grazing the cattle all day in the sun."

Rikku found a log and sat on it.

"I can guess where he's gone," he said. "He's gone to see what the medicine-man will do about my love-sickness." He laughed.

"Perhaps so, my son."

Leibe came from the hut and said, "Mother, won't you tell him about the three men I saw?"

"You saw three men?" Rikku put aside the bowl.

"Yes. They carried cages, and—and—birds!"

"Leibe!" said Shaitu sharply. "Go back and pound the corn." She turned to Rikku. "Do not mind your younger sister. She's only talking."

"But who were they?"

"Strangers. Bird-catchers, I think."

"And my father went with them?"

"Rikku, your questions are too many! Finish now and have your rest while I make supper. Is it not enough that your father is out and will soon be back?"

Shaitu went on with her husking and Rikku finished his meal in silence. He went inside the hut to take off his leather apron. She dared not let Rikku know what she secretly believed, that the *sokugo* was at work on his father. If Rikku believed that his father had gone to bring back the girl he loved, it was much better not to undeceive him.

* * *

Rikku woke in the small hours of the morning. Something, a slight unusualness in the air, had awakened him. He sat up with that immediate instinct of the nomad, developed over a lifetime of exposure to danger from man, beast and nature. It seemed to him that the cattle were milling around uneasily. He listened. No dogs were barking. But why? Had a spell been cast over them? He felt the restlessness spreading among the cattle. He heard real commotion now, as if someone was trying to stampede the bulls.

"Rikku!" Shaitu shouted from somewhere in the dark.

"Mother! Thieves . . . Get up. Thieves!"

A burst of uncontrolled movement shattered the night. Rikku slid under the door of the hut and out into the night. He saw a group of men—mere shapes—emerge from the darkness. The turbaned one was whispering commands, pointing. The other two in leather bags moved with precision, their daggers gleaming. They were cutting the cattle loose. From behind a pile of logs, Rikku watched them, crouching. Cattle stumbled blindly past him and crashed into the huts, whipped to recklessness by the shrieking orders of the men behind them. Rikku leapt aside, dodging a sharp object thrust at his ribs from behind. In an instant they had bound his hands behind his back, and made off. He heard his mother and the children screaming from the other hut, felt the choking smell of burning thatch followed by the sharp crackle of uncertain flames, then the whole settlement burst into one blinding sheet of flame, frightful to behold. His father's huts caught one spark; his mother's hut seemed to reach out a hand and to catch another flying spark. The sparks glowed in the wind, and soon those huts crackled alight.

"Leibe! Leibe!" Shaitu cried. "Rikku! Don't let Leibe burn to death."

"They have tied my hands!" Rikku yelled.

He saw the dark figures busy with the sinister work; flitting in and out of the cattle, cutting them loose, hurrying them away. Then in one final upward surge that dazzled the eyes, Rikku saw in the flaming mass the last indelible picture of his father's camp burning to ashes. He would never, as long as he lived, forget the choking smoke fumes drifting across the thorn, the upturned hoofs of the stampeding cattle, the red heart of the glowing fire that had once been a hut. He realised that the enemy had once again out-generalled him, and his heart sank. What remained deeply impressed in his memory was that face: a glimpse of it, dark, with a golden crest on the turban, catching the playing flames with now a dazzle, now a dull glow, and the tightly set teeth from which the commands issued.

The man was Ardo. Rikku knew of him; he had heard his father describe Ardo as his greatest rival for the chieftaincy of Dokan Toro. This man, Rikku remembered, had been seen in the afternoon by Leibe, releasing the dove with the talisman attached to its foot.

Did he aim to exterminate the entire family? If so, it must be true what Leibe had said that his father had been struck with the wandering disease and had not gone in quest of Fatimeh as Rikku had imagined but was merely wandering aimlessly over the veld. He must be pursued and saved.

Rikku worked his wrists, hoping to break the knots. But Ardo's men had done their work well.

CHAPTER FOUR

Mai Sunsaye kicked off his sandals, soaked his feet in the cool water and felt better.

"*Alla-ham-didil-lahi!*" he grunted with satisfaction. It was a meaningless expression, such as a man might make when he belches after a full meal. He bent down, keeping his clothes clear of the water. He washed his arms up to the elbows, massaged his facial muscles, and retired to a corner of the stream where he faced eastwards, and presently bowed to his Maker in the manner of really devout Muslims. Several hours later he was still there, tolling beads, and murmuring fervent prayers.

With half an eye to the east Mai Sunsaye watched the people who had now begun to come to the stream. Two lovely Fulani maids, their hair newly done, their bodies oiled, caught his immediate attention. They wore copper ear-rings, and as they set down their gourds of milk, a hundred bracelets glided smoothly down their long arms.

A donkey trudged down into the stream carrying a swaying load of sugar-cane. Other donkeys came, carrying yams. Sunsaye began to think; then it struck him that today was market day somewhere, that if he followed these people, he might get to a market. He was not really thinking of the dove any more, but he wanted to keep moving.

He finished his prayers and came down to a man who was making gurgling noises as he washed his throat.

"*San-nu!*" the man said. "Is it well with you?"

"It is well."

"Allah be praised, then!"

"I am asking for information," Sunsaye said.

"*Tau!*" the man said, which means 'good'. He stood up and thanked Allah.

"Yes," Sunsaye said. "You are going to market?"

"Just so."

"Perhaps I can go with you. My son Jalla may be there and I do not know the way."

The man hailed his donkey which had wandered away upstream where the grass was fresh, and presently it joined him. He put back the white brimless cap on his head, and smote the beast's hindquarters. Donkeys received no mercy, Sunsaye noted with pity.

"We go now," he said.

The tall slim girls had now finished their elaborate toilet and were rubbing their teeth with tobacco flower. Their lips were red, so were their teeth. Sunsaye was conscious of them as they climbed slowly up the bank of the stream. They were chatting excitedly and giggling as is the way with girls when they are together and gossiping.

Sunsaye looked far over the scrub and saw other groups of people converging on the market. They came from north, south, east and west, over the dry brown roads, and hurried over onwards to the grass huts that were the market stalls.

Fragments of the girls' conversation suddenly leapt into Sunsaye's ear. He was conscious of being unaccountably involved in what they were saying. With an absent-minded "yes" and "no" to the incessant chatter of his guide, he listened.

"Jalla! Ah, Jalla! *Wai!*" exclaimed one of the girls running some distance away and laughing while the other followed her with tossing aggression.

But the old man's restraint could hold out no longer. And when he heard one of them say: "You call Jalla like that, why? Do you then love him?" he went and spoke to them.

"Did I hear you say, Jalla, my pretty maids?"

The maidens looked at each other and at him with suspicion, balancing their trembling gourds on their heads gracefully.

"How is it?" one said.

"We were only playing," said the other.

"All is well," Sunsaye assured them. "I ask of him in peace."

They hesitated.

The darker one said, "Yes. We called Jalla."

"Then you know him?"

"Know him? The man from whom we buy our fresh milk and butter? Know him? Allah be praised!"

"Ah, how is an old man to know all that? I was merely asking, being a stranger to these parts."

"Wait . . . Jalla, he may even be in the market today. By

Allah, he should be. You know he loves finery. He must come to buy some ear-rings for . . ." They exchanged glances and burst out laughing.

Sunsaye's heart fell. So Jalla was married; or courting, and he had told no one. Sunsaye saw the man with the donkey waiting some distance ahead, his gnarled stick slung across his shoulders so that he rested his two wrists on the stick.

"We go now," he urged impatiently.

"We are coming!"

"You wanted to know something about Jalla?" said the man with the donkey. "Why did you not ask me? He who does not know Jalla in these parts must indeed be a stranger."

"I was merely——"

"Why, he is the favourite of the Bodejo. You don't know the Bodejo? *Kai!* But what kind of a man are you? There's not a man who does not know the Bodejo. He is a white man, and kind. You know? He gives injections to cattle. You hear me? Says the injection will save them from the rinderpest." And he roared with laughter, baring his tobacco-stained teeth.

The Bodejo, Dr. McMinter, was a vet., a Medical Officer of Health, and an upholder of British law and order, all thrown in one. But Mai Sunsaye could not ask too many questions without running the risk of disclosing that he was Jalla's father.

They emerged from the scrub, and the lone motor road lay before them, stretching right and left and disappearing in the hills. In the distance a cloud of dust indicated an approaching car. The reaction of the people about him terrified Sunsaye. The man with the donkey glanced about him uneasily as if in search of some hiding-place.

"It is the Bodejo," he said. "Quick! Do you want him to catch you and give you an injection? . . ."

"What shall we do?" cried the frightened maidens, grouping together like cattle.

The donkey owner now had his beast in check. "By Allah, if he sees us, we are for the needle."

"But you have not the sleeping sickness," Sunsaye pointed out. "I heard that he gives the needle only to people with the sleeping sickness."

The maidens cast their eyes about for some bush behind which to hide. There were none. An ostrich could have done better hiding in the desert. Amidst their panic the car dived into the valley. It seemed to sing as it took the hill. Its bonnet gleamed in the sun. With a whirr it was away. A trail of red dust hung all along the road and the wind was blowing it towards the frightened people.

"Did you see him?" whispered the donkey-man.

"He's a fine man!" the maidens sighed.

As they neared the market, Sunsaye noticed an official wearing a khaki helmet, stockings and boots in the manner of the tax-gatherers. He was standing amidst a number of herdsmen, and while they leaned on their sticks and watched him, he was talking and waving his arms.

"He is a Forest Officer," the donkey-man said. "His work is with the trees. Whatever the Bodejo wants done he tells Chikeh and then Chikeh tells us."

Sunsaye stood in respectful awe of the man with the note-book. But he was not too far away to hear a few words though they made no sense to him. The cattlemen were now dispersing. Some of them hung back to ask questions.

"I am still a cattleman," someone said. "My business is with cattle, not with wood."

This defiant speech was cheered by the cattlemen. Sunsaye's eyes widened with surprise. The loud-voiced young man was Jalla, his first son.

"There you make a mistake," the Forest Officer was saying. Sunsaye pushed and squeezed, thrusting himself forward to where Jalla was. All he wanted was to stand before his son. At last he stood before Jalla, now grown so big he had to crane his neck and speak to him from under a shadow.

"Jalla, my son!"

Jalla looked closely at the old man as if this were some revelation in a dream. "*Baba!*"

"*Lah, Lah, Lah!*" murmured the old man between embraces. They had stolen the show. The crowd, ever eager for a shameless exhibition of tender emotions, crowded around father and son. The maidens clasped their arms in sad rapture, extolling the joys of fatherhood.

"No wonder he's been asking about him," said one.

"Is that the old man we met at the stream? I suspected there was something."

Jalla turned to them and said proudly, "He is my father."

"*A-yah!* Poor old man. He has been trekking all day!"

Jalla and father stood looking at each other, a thousand unexpressed thoughts passing between them. Finally Jalla spoke. "We must go back now to the camp. It is many miles from here, but my horse can take us both. My boys will take the cattle home."

In Jalla's company Sunsaye walked through the market. It was crowded. All classes of people from all over the scrub had gathered, for it was held once a week. Shining combs from England were displayed side by side with roots and herbs and monkeys' teeth, and fly-ridden beef. Donkeys, cattle, *zana* matting; open fires with the meat sizzling; women with empty gourds, chewing sugar-cane. Donkeys, their forelegs tied with rope, hopped about picking sugar-cane skins with their lips.

"*Lah!*" Sunsaye kept saying.

He was proud of Jalla who did not look like a Fulani. Though he had nothing of their graceful effeminacy, Jalla wore ear-rings and a clean white jumper. His sandals were new because it was market day; or perhaps he had half an eye to some maiden. His mouth was red from chewing tobacco flower.

"*Lah!*" said the old man.

"Father, how is Rikku?"

"Rikku?" murmured Mai Sunsaye. "Rikku is sad, the little rascal! He is mooning over Fatimeh, a slave girl we rescued."

They did not get to Jalla's camp till late that night. Sunsaye could not see beyond the yellow circle of flame into the dark night, but he could hear the howl of the hyena in the rocks, and was vaguely aware of the outlines of white cattle, and brown ones.

He quickly found a mat and stretched his tired limbs.

"How many head have you?"

Jalla smiled. "Two hundred."

"Surely you are a great man, Jalla."

"It is Allah's will. Two hundred are here. But remember, one does not always want to pay the tax on all one has."

"You mean?"

"There are eight hundred in other places." He winked mischievously.

"*Wai! . . . Wai!*"

That night Sunsaye slept without turning round once. A day and a night separated him from Dokan Toro in a southerly direction, but he felt no desire to go back home, only forward.

A little after sunrise Sunsaye said he heard the rumbling of a car. He and Jalla listened. In the distance, a long red trail of dust marked the route of the machine. Some distance away from the camp it stopped and a white man stepped out of it. He was accompanied by an African in a khaki helmet, hose and boots. Together the two men strode over the low shrubs, talking and consulting notes.

"They're coming here," Sunsaye said. "Tax-gatherer!"

"It's the Bodejo. And the man with him is the Forest Officer of yesterday."

"What do they want? Tax money?"

"No!" Jalla smiled. "Let us wait and see."

The Bodejo approached with long strides. His assistant moved fast over the mounds of earth. He found the gate into the thorn fence, and in a moment he and the Bodejo were standing in the clearing. Mai Sunsaye had heard that the Doctor was a fine man, but being near him now he could well believe it. Dr. McMinter stood well over six foot six and had a smile like a Mexican. Yet in spite of his tan he seemed to carry that breath of England that made Sunsaye feel he was in contact with a new civilisation.

He looked over Jalla's herd.

"Any complaints?" he said.

Chikeh interpreted, and Jalla said, "None."

"Any recurrence of the rinderpest?"

"My Lord, since you gave them the injections, there has been so sign of it." He looked at his father. "*Kai!* . . . that disease! It nearly ate off all my cattle."

The Bodejo looked round the camp while Chikeh stood with them, making notes in a black book. Father and son regarded him mysteriously. He was an African like themselves, but unlike them he had been to school and could speak and write English. He rode a motor-cycle and in the bush he worked with complicated instruments.

The Bodejo appeared satisfied. He smiled warmly at Jalla, told him to report any suspicious symptoms, and with Chikeh walked back to the waiting car. Mai Sunsaye was still wrapped in admiration of his son.

"Jalla, you are the most important of my sons!"

"Why?"

"You ask me why? Just see how the Bodejo takes care of you and your cattle."

"He is a kind man." Jalla said. "His work is plentiful. He cures people of the sleeping sickness, he settles cases, he gives houses to the homeless. But——"

"*Tau!* What have you to say against him? Yes, of course, the tax." Sunsaye's face was grave. "One must face that. You are young and there is that blood of the rebel in you. But you can't run away for ever."

"It is so, father."

The Bodejo and the assistant had now reached their car in the distance. Sunsaye saw them both enter. The car began to move slowly, and again that red column of dust marked its trail.

"They have left!"

"Yes! They'll be back, though."

"Let us go and find something to eat. I am hungry.'

While they were gathering the firewood, Sunsaye said. "Jalla, is it not about time you had some maiden to do this for you?"

Jalla seemed not to have heard and Sunsaye repeated his question.

"Me?" said Jalla. "I had one, father. Amina was her name!"

"And where is she?"

"She ran away. It was after Hodio left here."

Sunsaye dropped the pile of wood. "Hodio! The same Hodio, my son? Where is Hodio now?"

"Father, I cannot tell. Some say he now has his own cattle and is roaming the wilds. Some say he has settled in the sleeping sickness camp. I forget the name. Wait! I believe it's called New Chanka."

"New Chanka; I've heard the name. There was Old Chanka which the Bodejo burnt, and now this New Chanka."

"Just so, father. But let us eat."

Jalla pounded some moist millet, added water in a pot

"Ah," said Jalla. "This is not a job for men."

and set it on the fire to boil. He squatted near it, watching with tearful eyes.

"Have you any flour?" Sunsaye said, with childlike enthusiasm.

"Everything is complete, except the fresh milk."

"We have that already," Sunsaye reminded him.

"Ah," said Jalla. "This is not a job for men."

Working together father and son got the meal ready. They drank the fluid with wooden spoons, chatting lightheartedly. By mid-morning Jalla said he would take the cattle downstream to graze. Sunsaye, fed to satisfaction, sat idly before the hut, gazing over the scrub.

Jalla looked at him and said: "Can I leave you with peace in my mind?"

"I go nowhere till I see you again," the old man said.

"But have you forgotten the *sokugo* that strikes without warning?"

Mai Sunsaye laughed. "There will be nothing, I assure you. Take your cattle to the stream. You will meet me here when you return."

"You will not run away on seeing a bird, or anything else on the wing? Father, I fear you really have the winged disease of the *sokugo*. And we have as yet consulted no medicine-man."

"Jalla, what is it you talk about so? D'you refer thus to your own father who gave you light?"

"I beg for mercy, father. It is fear that makes me talk thus. Great fear. Your manner brings on me this fear."

"I tell you I have come to look for the girl whom Rikku loves. Her name is Fatimeh. And——"

"Is that so?" Jalla smiled.

"But, by Allah. On my way I heard talk about you, Jalla, so I followed the maidens and the man on the donkey."

"*Tau!* So you say, and so be it! I'll go and leave you here. The sun rises higher. Soon the grass will be too dry."

"Go in peace." He stroked his beard and murmured into it. "All those muscles! He does not look like our slender, graceful Fulani son."

The cattle mooed. The wide span of their sweeping horns clacked against one another. Their humps danced. This was always the most difficult part of it, arousing them from their lethargy and getting them moving. Once they understood what was afoot it was not so difficult. But the smaller ones would always be in the way. Jalla lashed out with his whip. "*Kai!*" He made clucking noises with his tongue, bullying this, calling out to that one by name. A good herdsman must know each one of his cattle by name, colour and habits.

Sunsaye smiled at his son's expert herdsmanship. In a short while Jalla had manœuvred them all into the old cattle trails and now stood apart from them, leaning on a stick, whistling and cajoling while the cattle moved lazily streamwards. Jalla took a swig at his flask and joined them.

"Wait for me, father," he hailed. "I'll be back at sundown."

Mai Sunsaye rose and waved at him. "Allah bless you, my son!"

Jalla urged them into the stream, standing apart and watching them splash.

CHAPTER FIVE

The cattle waded into the stream before him and he let them find their own way, retiring to a little hill some distance away. From here he could see them spread along either bank and along the flat grassland adjoining. They knew the land as well as he did, and he settled down and watched them. When the sun began to slant overhead behind the rocks, he would take them round through Dogo's farm. Dogo always liked their droppings.

Jalla sat with his knees wide apart, his hands resting on the stick. His eyes roved far and away over the grassland. It was odd the way this big patch of scrub seemed to behave. On market days, all the roads would be full, but on days like this the sun beat down on the grass and thorn trees, the gardenias, and not a soul disturbed the burning paths. The grass here was becoming sour. He must think of moving camp soon. He would go northwards and seek the river banks.

Presently he thought he could detect a movement in the distance, and looking more closely, found that two figures had broken the outline of the horizon. They were both hooded and approached with a certain amount of pain and effort.

Jalla regarded them without interest. There were a lot of bush dwellers in the scrub, and one could not bother too much with them. But then he noticed that one of the figures was a woman, and the smaller one a child. They were chatting and pointing, and presently they turned away and vanished behind a bush.

Towards dusk Jalla gathered his herd and directed them slowly back to the camp. He was pleased when he saw the two huts with their happy promise of the old man's appreciative smile. He coralled his cattle, and went indoors. Mai Sunsaye was not in the room. He examined the next hut. What he saw made him jump back: a woman with a child was lying on the mat fast asleep. Beside her lay a little girl.

He went in and shook her by the shoulder. "*Kai!* What's up?"

She started and opened her eyes. "Who?"

Then Jalla saw her face. "My mother!" he exclaimed, striking his breast. "Allah descend from above!"

"Jalla, my own!"

"How is it, mother? Who showed you the way?"

Leibe stirred and he took her in his arms. "My dear sister! You are becoming a woman now!" He plucked at her cheeks.

"Yes," said Shaitu. "She was betrothed three years ago. Thanks to Allah you are so well known here, Jalla. I kept asking of you and they showed me this hut."

"Oh, mother! Now that I see you, my heart is indeed gladdened. . . ."

She smiled affectionately. "Did your father come this way? He ran away from home, and——"

"Is that why you are here?"

"Just so. We have been on the road for three days . . . Not a morsel have we eaten."

"Don't worry! There is food in plenty and you will soon see my father." He went out and from the door said: "It must have been you I saw this afternoon."

"You were with the cattle?"

"*Ai!* I saw you. Two of you, and I wondered. But I thought you were going somewhere. Now I must make you some food, and soon Mai Sunsaye will be back. I believe——"

"He was here, then?" Shaitu said eagerly.

"*Wal-lah-hi!* The man you seek is in the camp somewhere."

"We did not meet him."

Jalla's heart sank. He dared not think of it. It could not be. A dryness was coming to his throat. "You—did—not meet him?"

"Not even his sandals. *Wal-lah-hi!*"

"Allah forbid it. No, I'm sure he will soon be——"

But even as they set out to search for him in the neighbourhood, Jalla feared the worst. He kept suggesting that the old man must have gone in search of a root, a herb, but then looking more closely he found nothing to indicate that his father proposed to return.

"He is gone," he sighed. Then as if speaking to himself, "That disease, the *sokugo*."

"You know, then?"

"I suspected it; but he told me he is in search of Fatimeh. I do not know what to believe."

Shaitu was silent. Dusk was setting over the scrub as they walked back to the camp. Leibe, sucking her hand, looked up at her big brother.

"They burnt our house," she said. "They beat us. I believe they ran away with Rikku. Allah will send down a curse on them!" She was sobbing now.

"But I did not know all this! When did it happen?"

"On the night Mai Sunsaye left. Yet if you knew, Jalla, what would you do? You are so far away from us. Three days' journey. And there is so much on your hands."

"That is true, mother; but something must be done. We must find Rikku, and stop our father from following this shadow of things that fly."

In the evening they sat by the fire, and Jalla's joy was great at tasting his mother's cooking. He looked at her now, still beautiful in her middle age. She was so selfless, yet life had somehow not been entirely kind to her. He felt he must do something, however little, to make life more comfortable for her.

"I enjoyed that," he said, scooping the rice with his fingers. "You should have tasted the paturi that father and I made this morning!"

"Was it sweet?" Leibe asked.

"Sweet, by Allah!" and he laughed.

Leibe smiled. "But you kept none for us."

"Did I know you were coming? Now what about Rikku? I wish he too were here."

"We haven't seen him, Jalla, my son. When the leaves

were burning I had to take the baby and also Leibe. I looked for Rikku, but did not find him."

"Perhaps Ardo's men took him," Leibe said.

"Nothing will happen to my son! Allah help him to win through! Nothing will happen to him! I know Rikku. If they have taken him, I'm sure he will find a way to escape. Those wicked people!"

After dinner they sat by the fire and talked It was very late indeed when a tired figure salaamed and Shaitu and Jalla looked up. Rikku was standing there. He was leaning on a stick and looked on the verge of collapse. When he walked towards them, it was with a limp and he was quiet and unsmiling. His face was scarred and swollen. They ran towards him.

"Rikku, my son! Allah has saved you for me. Let me have your bag, and your stick. Come, there's a little rice and butter left. And some hot water."

Rikku followed his mother and sat down on a goat-skin. When the food was brought he ate hungrily.

"Who showed you the way?"

"People of the scrub."

"I am glad indeed, Rikku. Let us boil you some water. When you have bathed I shall dress your burn."

"Thank you, mother."

While he ate, his strength seemed to return. He began to tell them how Ardo's men, having taken all they wanted, knocked him unconscious and threw him near one of the burning huts. Here he had been picked up by a man who came to see Sunsaye.

"But I was determined to set off after them. Then on the

way I asked about you and they showed me this place. Jalla, everyone on the veld knows you. I am indeed proud." He called for a bowl of water and washed his hands. "You see that Ardo? He will not last long as a chief. He believes in force. Already the people are grumbling. If our father had been there!"

"We must find him!" said Shaitu.

Before he went to bed, Rikku called Jalla aside.

"Jalla, you have prospered."

"Allah be praised," said Jalla. "All prosperity is from above."

"Brother. There's something. About our father."

"Yes," said Jalla. Rikku looked him in the eye. "You know what I am going to ask. Do you think he is—well?"

Jalla sighed. "My brother, it is hard indeed to tell. It is hard. Sometimes he acts like one who has the *sokugo*. But remember he is not a young man and he loves you much!"

He would not say more and Rikku looked at him again then turned towards the sleeping-hut.

CHAPTER SIX

Sweat lay on Mai Sunsaye's arms like flecks of foam. A warm glow pervaded his limbs, making them tingle. But he was getting exhausted. Over the veld, the vertical rays of the sun shimmered, creating mirages. The sight of a clump of thatch gave him fresh courage.

As he drew nearer the wall round the village became more distinct and beyond it towered a giant baobab tree, twisting its knotty and leafless branches against the sheer blue sky. In the darker trees, the white cattle egrets and vultures battled with noisy flaps of their wings.

Village walls and trees showed some promise of life and from the sight of them he drew fresh courage. He quickened his pace. His sandals click-clacked behind him and the dust rose, caking his feet, till he longed for somewhere cool and shady where he could wash and say his noon prayers.

What he had seen was indeed a town wall, about waist high, but still a wall. Inside it were mud huts, roofless. It struck him as odd, and as he came nearer he noticed too that even the town wall seemed to have been broken down in parts. This was a spectacle of desolation.

He entered by a broad path flanked by two large baobab trees. The wheels of a motor vehicle were still fairly fresh, and it seemed to him that he could smell the petrol and the dust. As soon as he set foot within the gate a voice challenged him. "Mallam!"

Sunsaye turned. At first he saw no one. Looking more cautiously he noticed a man who was so dirty that he seemed to merge into the dust. His shrunken arm gripped a cudgel and his eyes glinted ferociously.

"May you be greeted," Sunsaye said, wondering what he had done wrong.

A stealthy movement like a snake brought the man nearer. "Where are you going, my son?"

"Me?" said Mai Sunsaye. He had not been called 'my son' for more than twenty years. "I am going into the village."

The old man laughed. "The village! He, he, heee! . . . The village!" His laughter was chilling.

Sunsaye, irritated, turned abruptly and made a move to resume his journey. As he walked on, he had an idea that something uncanny awaited him. In his ears still rang the cackle of the old man's chilly laugh. It was real enough this noon. At night he might have dismissed it as a mere flight of fancy.

The first house he came to had no roof, and showed signs of having been burnt down. In the other houses, there were cobwebs. Rats came out by day and stood on their hind legs, washing their hands like humans. He walked on. Everywhere the signs of desolation increased. Market-places with caved-in stalls, their floors strewn with wrapping leaves. Broken pots still holding a little water in which the mosquitoes bred freely; spoons, chairs, rusty tins, sugar-cane peelings, donkey hoof-marks.

He could even see the ashes of the fire where the butchers were wont to sizzle beef on sticks and sell to the young men. But where were the butchers and the farmers and the blacksmiths? Were they dead, buried, drowned out by some flood or burnt to ashes?

He stood there, baffled and bewildered. Close behind him, he heard a stealthy movement. He turned round just in time. The twisted old face and downward-swinging cudgel flashed past him. The air was thick with the odour of the man's unwashed body.

"*Kai!*" Sunsaye drew in his breath. "How now? A man has done nothing to you and you attack him from the back, like a cowardly old woman?"

"You've done nothing? You trespasser!"

The man with the club picked himself up and sprang again at Mai Sunsaye. This time he landed a stinging blow on the neck of the herdsman, drawing blood. Mai Sunsaye saw the blood on his gown, and he was glad. The *sharro* test had trained him never to flinch at the sight of blood. Was he not a one-time champion of that bloody sport at which a man takes a flogging that he might prove his courage?

He stood now with feet astride, rolling up one leg of his trousers. As the old man lunged yet again, Mai Sunsaye leapt into the air. He swung a leg over the man's head, missed and was sent spinning into the bush.

He got up, panting. "Baba! I warn you. You are

near the grave; it shall not be my doing that will put you inside. So, please beware!"

"Get back the way you came!" the old man panted. "Go away now! I want no stranger in my kingdom." He began to laugh, holding his sides. "You think it is not my kingdom? Ha, ha! Yes, everybody has deserted. They are afraid of the sleeping sickness. But not me! The flies can suck my dry blood, and they shall die!"

Mai Sunsaye let fall his trouser leg. He glanced over his shoulder and said, "By Allah! I do not know what to make of you. Sometimes I think you are mad. But why must you hurt me? I am a passer-by on my way through your village. I do not mean to rob you of your kingdom."

"You wanted it that way. But let's forget it. In the name of the Prophet, have you any kola? I am hungry."

Mai Sunsaye drew up his robe and from knee-deep pockets produced a dried and shrivelled nut. He offered it to his assailant. Baba chewed off a little bit, made a face, and licked his lips.

"A good nut, this!"

Mai Sunsaye was still busy with his wound. "Where can I find water?"

"Water? There, down by the stream."

"Take me there."

As they walked on, Mai Sunsaye could not help reflecting on how much better a friend some men became if you got to know them over a fight. There were more and more signs of desolation all over the village. Baba noticed his curiosity and asked: "You have come to look for someone?"

"That is so."

"Ah! You have come too late—too late!"

"How? Has there been a war here?"

"Not a war. But then, it was a war. When the forest burns do the locusts stop to say goodbye?"

"I do not see that so well——"

"*Tau!*" Baba laughed. "I say there has been a war. If a fish comes out of the water and says the crocodile has one eye, who has been there with him?"

"No one but Allah," Sunsaye grinned, warming to the man's proverb. Truly, this man could be amusing.

"There has been a war! You are in your own house, where you were born and your father before you. An officer of the Government comes and says it is not good for you. It is full of sickness. He burns or breaks down your house, and builds you another, far away, in another land. *Tau!*"

Mai Sunsaye paused. An irritation at the back of his left arm made him turn it slowly. As he had suspected, an insect had been biting him. It was a large fly, and its wings were folded at the back like a pair of scissors. Its abdomen was swollen and still swelling and red with his blood. Mai Sunsaye, shivering, raised his arm to strike.

"Kill it!" shouted Baba. "It is the tsetse fly!"

Baba sprang forward excitedly, flourishing his arm. Before either of them could strike, the fly rolled over and lay in the dust, too heavy even to fly away. Baba leapt at it as if he were trampling down an elephant. Not until the blood had mixed with the earth did he wipe the sweat running down his wrinkled face.

"That was the cause of the war!" he said.

"The fly?"

"It is the tsetse. It causes the sleeping sickness."

He held Mai Sunsaye by the hand and led him on. The stream was practically dry, because most of the trees had been cut down along its banks. The grass was making a vague attempt to remain green.

"All these places," Baba said, sitting on a stone, "were once inhabited by people like you and me. Farmers and their wives, traders. They were happy but full of sickness."

Mai Sunsaye was making gurgling noises. He washed and rinsed his mouth, spat out the water, then washed his dry, dusty feet.

"You, Baba. Tell me, what is your mission here?"

"Listen to a question! Ha, ha! To see a man in his own home and then to ask him—*Kai!*"

"But the officers say no man shall remain here."

Baba laughed. "Where is the business of the fish with the tick? Am I too young to die? If the sickness catches me, let me die!"

"Come," said Mai Sunsaye, "it is time for prayers."

The old man came down the bank of the stream. After his ablutions, both men faced East, and the older man showed that he could be as devout as he was vicious and unpredictable. He had a deep voice which he apparently reserved for moments such as this, and Sunsaye was deeply moved.

"Amin," said Sunsaye, wiping the sand off his brow and producing his chaplet.

Baba said, "And now, what are your plans?"

"I turn my face to the south."

"Truly? That is good; by Allah, that is good. But then you cannot proceed today. Already night is coming. Time for the hyenas and bad beasts of the scrub to be abroad."

"You speak truth."

"Will you come with me and rest here for the night?"

Mai Sunsaye remembered the unprovoked attack of the afternoon and hesitated. This might be another trap. Night might convert the old devil into a fiend. On the other hand; those eyes of Baba's, transparent brown and too brilliant for a man of his own age, they revealed nothing. The cunning smile was an enigma. Mai Sunsaye gazed at the expressionless face and was tantalised.

"Shall we go?" said Baba.

"Lead on," said Sunsaye, with sudden decision. He had just looked at the sky and the white flecks of cloud were coming together and darkening into grey. If it did not rain shortly, it might, later on.

Baba's house amused Mai Sunsaye. It was one of the abandoned huts, roofless and curiously damp. Baba had made futile attempts to pull a roof over it, but the only comfort came from a baobab tree near by with a log at the bottom of it. Mai Sunsaye sat here, while the old man made a hasty meal of kneaded flour steeped in sour milk.

"Where did you buy the flour?" Sunsaye asked.

"There! In the village of New Chanka. That's what they call the one they built to replace Old Chanka, where we are now."

"How far away is it?"

"Not far. A lazy man, leaving here at dawn, in the

wetness of the dew, will get to New Chanka before the sun is over our heads.

"*Tau!*"

"Sometimes, I go there," Baba said. "But the place is too clean for me. Too clean! Even their wells have cement floors, and the market too. *Kai!*"

"You will show me the way tomorrow?"

"That is not difficult. But, by Allah, you are not leaving tomorrow?"

"*Wal-lahi!* Tomorrow I must leave. I am in quest of something."

"A man?"

"No. A fair maiden. Indeed, as lovely a maiden as my son deserves."

"Ho?" breathed Baba. He set about making a fire. As he broke the sticks, he said, "A maiden is one of those things a man must not trust. By Allah, it is!"

"And the others?"

"A prince, a river, a knife, and darkness. A prince because his word changes with the weather; a river because in the morning you may wade across it, but in the evening it has swollen and can swallow you. A knife, because it knows not who carries it. Darkness, ha! Who knows what lurks in it. Certainly, all evil things."

"Whatever may be the case, Baba, when day breaks, my journey resumes. I must think of the boy."

They soon got a meal ready: sweet potatoes, toasted peanuts. Sunsaye, being Fulani, would not eat the meat from cattle: it was forbidden by herdsmen. Baba was sorry he had nothing else in his larder. They ate the kneaded flour in sour milk first; then they fell to, savouring the sweet potatoes. When darkness fell, both men were so tired that they went to their sleeping places without waiting. Mai Sunsaye lay on a mat, and watched Baba potter about. Truly, a mad man. Quick to fight, quicker still to make friends. But would he remain friendly till dawn?

CHAPTER SEVEN

Mai Sunsaye did not move for a week. Between him and Baba had developed a new friendship nurtured by strange comforts they discovered together in the city of ruins. Like boys they wandered about Old Chanka by day, and by night they sat around the fire and talked.

One morning, Mai Sunsaye went down to the stream, washed his eyes and feet in the ice-cold water and came back to Baba's hut. He found Baba plucking the feathers off a partridge he had shot that morning.

"Baba, it is time to thank you for all your kindness. May Allah bless you and shower you with much happiness in your little village. But now, I must be going."

"No, Mai Sunsaye! I have grown too fond of you."

"Such is life: meeting and parting."

"Truly. None the less it is never sweet to part."

"I wish to set out, because my heart has become heavy within me. By Allah, I have tried to be happy here, but must I neglect the object of my quest? You know how it is when a father loves his son as well as I love Rikku."

"Do I know? *Wal-lahi!* I had a son I loved. But he was

a headstrong one, and he got up and went to the wars of the white men. He said he would come back but I have not seen him since."

"Truly, a brave lad!"

"Brave! Ha, he was a mad one. When the white men came to this village, it was still thriving and full of people. That was the Old Chanka! The soldiers played their music and showed us their guns. They asked for volunteers to fight the war.

They made big promises. Free food, fine uniforms. Free passage to distant lands over the seas. My dear Mallam, I swear to you that had I been a young man then nothing would have stopped me. The madness of it! But alas! my bones were stiff, and they would not take me. My son Shehu went with them, and to this day, he is still not back." Tears stood in Baba's eyes.

"Allah descend from heaven," Sunsaye said, striking his breast. "But so many died, and so many returned. It is impossible to be quite sure."

"May Allah's mercy descend upon us."

"Amin!"

Both men observed a moment's silence. Sunsaye lifted his eyes and looked squarely at Baba's face. "I go now!" They shook hands.

Mai Sunsaye set off, arriving at New Chanka in the early afternoon. The village was quite unlike the Old Chanka he had left behind him. There was no town wall. The huts were built in a rectangle, and young mango and orange trees had been planted in every courtyard. No baobabs. Sunsaye, unable to repress his excitement, hurried eagerly forward.

Little boys and girls winding out bucketfuls of water from the wells took no notice of him.

As he approached one of the houses, he saw a man whipping a horse which went round and round. The horse tugged at a crude capstan, while the man urged it on. Sunsaye could not understand what man and horse could be working at, but he thought the man might be able to help him in his quest.

"Hail!" he shouted.

The man turned. The horse swung round, nearly butting him down. He held the reins and checked it.

"May you be greeted!"

Sunsaye could see the sudden knotting up of the young man's brow. Beneath the fine layer of sweat something seemed to leap alive. Sunsaye himself experienced a curious feeling. His throat became suddenly parched as if he had been thirsty for weeks. He took a few paces forward, then halted.

"Hodio, my son!" He raised his arms. "Can it be you?"

"Father!"

"Greet me. Greet me!"

The big boy ran and embraced his father so hard that the old man cried out in pain.

"By Allah," Mai Sunsaye said. "If I had set out to discover all my sons, instead of questing for Fatimeh——"

Hodio's hands dropped cold. The old man searched his face. "What's wrong, my son?"

"Nothing."

"You are hiding something from me. I feel it!"

Hodio was silent. His father felt a sharp pang, more painful than a dagger thrust. "Then, you are not pleased I came?"

"It's not that, father. Is mother well?"

"Your mother? Er—yes, yes!"

Hodio said, "Why do you answer in that way? If she is ill, let me know. Was that why you came?"

"She is well," said Sunsaye. "I swear she is."

"I am making sugar," Hodio said, leading him towards the capstan. "In this village of New Chanka, anyone may learn to make sugar if he has a little money and can buy a mill. It is the way they plan to make us like the place. You see, this machine costs twenty-five pounds. It crushes the sugar-cane and the juice flows out."

"How do you work it?" Sunsaye asked, fascinated.

Hodio smiled proudly. "Draw back a little. I'll show you."

He whipped the horse and Mai Sunsaye saw that it had been cunningly harnessed to a mill. Sugar-cane was fed in from one end and as the horse ran round and round, supplying the power, the foaming juice rushed out into a large tin.

"*Lah!*" exclaimed Sunsaye, well pleased.

"I am going to light a fire soon," Hodio told him proudly. "And then I shall cook this juice till it is thick. *Wal-lahi!* I think I am ready now."

He stopped the horse, unharnessed it, and allowed it to graze. He lighted the fire, and while the juice cooked talked about his brothers.

"Rikku?" Mai Sunsaye told him. "I left him at Dokan Toro with his mother; so is Leibe. She is growing into quite a maiden now! But Jalla! He has prospered best of you all. He has one thousand head of cattle. I stopped with him at his camp."

"One thousand!"

"Yes, Hodio. He is not like you. Jalla was patient, biding his time."

"By the way, did he mention Amina to you?"

"Who is Amina?"

"Then you do not know?" Hodio sighed. He was very relieved. "Amina was the girl Jalla set his heart upon. But —I took her away from him and we fled here."

"You should not have done so. Your own brother!"

"But, father, it is legal. Custom says that a woman is no wife, till she is brought under the hut. And I captured Amina before she became a bride. So, by custom, she is mine!"

"And Fatimeh, the slave girl with whom you ran away? Where is she? What has become of her?"

Hodio stared at his father. His face twitched, just before he turned and began to blow the fire with the leather bellows. He straightened up and stood staring at the roaring flames.

"Very soon it will boil," he said.

"So?"

Mai Sunsaye ventured much nearer and dipped his finger into the froth. He licked it, rolled his tongue over his thin lips, then stared at Hodio for a time. Hodio was a wiry young man with legs slender and springy as an antelope's.

"It is like sugar-cane."

Hodio laughed. "It *is* sugar-cane; what else? You saw

the canes a moment ago! This is the juice squeezed out from them."

"But how will this become sugar such as a man might melt in his pap?"

"That one is easy. When the fire is truly ablaze, the liquid will thicken. It will thicken and thicken, until it is almost like kneaded flour; then I'll pour it into moulds. When it sets, it is ready."

Mai Sunsaye nodded in appreciation.

"At last you have learnt a useful trade, and one that might calm down your restlessness. But, Hodio, how long have you been at it?"

"Since I left home. But at first, I was too happy with Fatimeh to worry about work. It was after that fight——"

"So there *was* something you were hiding! You fought with Fatimeh, and——"

"Not with her, no! Allah forbid that!" His eyes blazed with sudden defiance. "The man who owned her came after me with two ruffians. They overpowered me and snatched her away. See!" He lifted his trousers. "You see that wound? It is slowly healing. Even now, I feel it ache when I bend down. Shehu gave me that wound. The ruffian!"

"Shehu, you said?"

"Yes, Shehu. Why do you scratch your beard? Do you remember him? No doubt you do! You remember the evening when Fatimeh came running to us and his servant pursued her? Oh now, we did not see Shehu then, only the servant. When we bought Fatimeh for five cattle, Shehu was not there. Well, I heard of this village, New Chanka.

The white men and the Medical people were moving the villagers from the Old Chanka to New Chanka. All because of the fly that gives men the sleeping sickness. So I came here with them. I heard about the sugar-cane mill and they helped me to buy this one. I pay back money every month from what I earn. Some day it will be my own, with nothing more to pay. Then I can live like a town dweller."

Sunsaye shook his head in disapproval. "You have given up cattle, just for this? You whom I brought up with the cattle in your veins?"

Hodio laughed. "The choice was made for me, after what I had done to Rikku and to Jalla."

He poured the thick syrup into moulds and set them to dry in an oven which he locked up.

"Tomorrow they will be ready. I'll get the horse and we'll go home. I am very tired."

"Hodio's house was situated at the back of the settlement. Like the others it was a mud hut, neatly thatched and well white-washed.

Hodio raised the *zana* curtain over the front door.

"There is no guinea-worm in the water here," he said, as Sunsaye stooped and entered. It was dark inside until Hodio opened the windows.

"The flies that bring the sickness have never bitten anyone. That is because the health workers have cut away all heavy trees round New Chanka. In this town too there is a place where a man with the sleeping sickness may go for treatment."

"It is too clean," Sunsaye grumbled. He looked through

the window, at houses geometrically laid out, each one standing a good distance away from the next house, each one with the same number of guava trees and orange trees. He remembered what Baba meant when he said he could not stand the antiseptic cleanliness. "There is no smell of cattle-dung. It is like a hospital. A town must have the smell of cattle to please a Fulani."

Hodio laughed. Mai Sunsaye sat on a leopard-skin on the floor, his eyes roving round the room. He felt like one in another world. Hodio moved about like a stranger. It was difficult to imagine that this slim athletic boy in so modern a town was his own son.

"My wife, Amina, is not back. She's gone to sell sweets and milk in the town near by."

Mai Sunsaye noticed a large collection of Arabic writing, bound in leather, and lying in stacks against the wall. He smiled. Hodio was at last turning his thoughts to religion and righteous living.

He reached out, and taking one of the books began to examine it with interest. A vein was throbbing in his head. The characters began to dance with staggering unrest before his eyes. He placed a hand against his brow and noticed that it was very hot. The fever had come. He remembered the fly that had bitten him yesterday and was terrified. Had he got the sleeping sickness?

In less than an hour he was on his back, wrapped in the thickest clothes. He was shivering and blubbering in his delirium, and could feel and smell the shea butter as Hodio rubbed it over his eyes.

"Hodio, Hodio, I die——"

"May Allah come down in mercy. That will not happen here."

"Amin! Amin!"

Mai Sunsaye heard the word sweetly said by a soft voice at his bedside.

"My wife Amina," Hodio told him. "But you have strained yourself too much in your wanderings. Lie down and be calm. You are not so young as before."

"I know. It is old age. My time is up."

Hodio handed him a concoction which he sipped greedily. When he woke, he was alone. He had been having a nightmare. The night was very still and so silent he could hear the crickets chirp. Amina told him that Hodio had left New Chanka in pursuit of Shehu. The man who had snatched Fatimeh from him had suddenly appeared in the village.

"When will he be back?"

"My husband's father, I cannot tell."

"It is stupid! Suppose they ambush him? Oh, by Allah! pray to Allah! Give him the calmness of mind. Let him turn back and come home to us." His lips moved in prayer and soon his head was drooping and the sound of his snoring filled the room.

CHAPTER EIGHT

Hodio's gallop out of New Chanka quickened as his temper mounted. He dug his heels hard into his horse's flanks, cursing the while, slashing cruelly down with his cane. Lying close to his horse's mane, his eyes darted keenly into every nook and crevice of the scrub.

The scrub was practically empty, except for one or two stragglers, farmers who reared their heads, hoe in hand, to squint at him. A thicket would sometimes look like a man, but it was only an illusion. The grass swayed before the wind, the little wiry trees dotted the fields.

His horse twisted and turned as it followed the crooked path before him. Shehu and his men had had too much of a start. At this rate, he might never catch up with them. A gazelle darted across his path. Happy hunting it would have been at other times, but not now.

Now he was completely clear of New Chanka and the countryside had changed into uncultivated bush. On both sides, the leafless trees were mustering against him, obscuring his vision. The footprints on the path multiplied till they became millions: four-toed dents super-imposed on broader soles, starry imprints of birds' feet chequered the bigger pug-marks of the hyena.

He slowed down. The large rock ahead of him would bear no prints. But something else seemed imminent. He could almost feel a third presence. He got down, climbed the large rock. From the top he commanded a grand view of the country behind him. It was a dead end, true enough. But somewhere behind this rock should be another path. It might take long to find, perhaps too long.

He decided to search. He turned. Like a flash, the arrows whizzed past his ear. He threw himself flat down. His horse broke away, yelping with pain. He could see the butts of at least three arrows in its flank. Slowly the horse would die of the poison in the iron tips.

He looked down the bottom of the rock and saw three men labouring up towards him. The biggest of them all was Shehu, the man he sought. Shehu, master of the girl Fatimeh: original cause of the split in the Sunsaye family.

Hodio whipped out his dagger from a belt fastened to his forearm. It seemed to him now that something was coming to an end, and very soon too. The men's swords slapped against their legs as they clambered. So swords would be the weapons! He drew his. And there he stood on the bare rock, a dagger in one hand, a sword in the other, waiting. And beyond him, out of human sight, was New Chanka, and Amina. He had stolen Amina, and now he was prepared to die for Fatimeh. He knew he had no chance against the three of them, but he would show them yet.

He heard Shehu laughing, "Ha, ha, ha!" A hoarse satisfied laugh that told of gallons of corn beer.

He felt the cold chill of helplessness run down his back. He was alone, out among his enemies. "No, we shall not kill him—yet!" said one of the men.

Shehu did not draw his sword; he was puffing slightly and he stopped a good distance away from Hodio. Quietly he took out a bow and studiously selected a good-bladed arrow. Hodio could see his hands clearly: large, very black and steady. His glossy moustache and goatee beard gave an unrelenting firmness to his already vicious look.

"You dirty thief!" he snarled. "Prepare now for the slow death of a thief!"

Hodio, lashed to anger, stood at bay. He felt the net closing around him, felt his complete powerlessness.

"You still would not heed my warning," Shehu went on. "Such fools as you should be quartered and left to the vultures to devour. No, to the hyenas! It is not enough to send my slaves to beat you up!"

"Worthless talk!" Hodio interrupted impatiently. "Listen! I am Hodio, son of Sunsaye of the cattle Fulani. My father makes darkness for his enemies. *Yee-whoo!*" He leapt backwards screaming. From his pocket he drew a talisman of black catskin and waved it. This was the *baduhu*, known throughout the savannah lands as the Giver of Darkness. Hodio threw it down on the rock between him and his enemies. "He who crosses that, falls into a well. *Wai!* You dare to measure your might against the magic of a cow Fulani, son of Sunsaye the famous medicine man? Come now and meet your doom!"

The three men gazed doubtfully at one another. It was no fable, what Hodio had said. The Fulani were well known in Northern Nigeria for their magic. By magic they camp without a fence and no lion dare seize a beast. By magic and superstition they live and die.

"On him, fools!" shouted Shehu, ignoring the warning.

Hodio sneered. "Come into the well that gives darkness to the eyes and confounds the senses. Come into the darkness that weakens the limbs. *Ai!* I am Hodio, son of Sunsaye. We are Fulanis, sons of Dan Fodio, master magicians, we who fight like cats, who die a hundred deaths and live, we who test our manhood by the *sharro*—"

"Do you listen to that babble, you dogs?" Shehu growled.

The first man lunged at Hodio, seemed to buckle and falter. His tongue lolled out suddenly and he stared about him with a helpless look. Hodio slashed at the man's back with his sword, wounding him. The other man turned and fled.

Shehu alone stood his ground. "You are a coward to fight me with magic. Come for what you're worth and let me teach you a lesson."

Hodio picked up the catskin, the giver of darkness, and held it in one hand. Their engagement was short and noisy with the clash of weapons. Hodio felt a sharp stab of pain in his thigh, reopening an old wound. He struck back, catching Shehu on the back of the arm.

"Let us go!" his men called out.

"I must kill him first," Shehu shouted back with spirit.

But Hodio kept up his magic chant, gazing with fire into the eyes of Shehu. And Shehu was weakening. Hodio forced him down the hill until he turned and fled towards his waiting horse. There was a sudden scurrying of feet as their horses broke cover and galloped over the veld.

Left alone, Hodio went back to his horse. It was quite dead. He cut off the tail, removed the saddle and, murmuring a quiet blessing, started his homeward journey.

Hodio struggled back to New Chanka. He saw Amina sitting up waiting for him. Amina ran towards him and took the saddle from his hands.

"Hodio! Welcome!"

"You are well? You have not been fighting? We have been so worried about you. Your father wanted to come after you."

"I am quite well. How is father? Is he better now?"

He raised the *zana* matting and entered the room. His father was sitting with his back against the wall, smiling thinly.

"Welcome, son."

"Allah welcomes us. Those devils! By Allah's help, I shall one day face Shehu man to man! They were three. But I showed them! *Yee-whoo!* The *baduhu* that father gave me!" He saw the proud smile on his father's face. "Yes, he will learn what it is to fight against a cow Fulani."

But it seemed to him that his father and his wife were more delighted to see him back than to hear stories of his exploits. Soon he had a bath and a meal, and he and his father sat talking after Amina had retired.

"He who waits will see what is in the grass," Hodio said. "I plan to remain here at New Chanka and to follow this sugar making. If I stay here two or three years, I shall be something. Oh, yes!"

He talked with real fire and he saw the look of surprise and pleasure in his father's face.

"Whenever you need any help, you must send for me," Hodio told his father. "I am your son, and I am at your command."

"All help comes from above," Sunsaye said. "I shall remember."

On the morning following it was market day. Hodio and Amina went early to the market, leaving Sunsaye on the mat. When they returned from the market in the evening, the old man was gone and no one could tell them where.

CHAPTER NINE

Night had fallen over Jalla's camp and with it came a feeling of gloom, for Jalla was proposing to strike camp and travel south to Malendo. With heavy hands Shaitu and Leibe were churning the sour milk near the huts, their ears tuned to the conversation of Jalla and Rikku.

"We shall split the herd in two," Jalla suggested. This was an old ruse, to foil the tax-gatherers who might waylay them. "Rikku, you will go with some cattle to Ligu's camp. I shall give you a man, a good man too."

Jalla looked at his mother, and said: "Shaitu, you and Leibe and the little one will come with me. We shall go to Malendo near the gold mines. It is twenty days' trek from here. There we shall stop till the grass is sour. If all is well, Rikku will join us there."

Shaitu said, "By Allah's help, all will be well. But, Jalla, shall we see Mai Sunsaye?"

"*Wal-lahi*, my mother. You talk as but a child. If Allah wills, we shall find him. If not, then we must be content till he himself returns to us. He is not lost to us!"

"Then you do not believe that he has the *sokugo*?"

"I do not know what to believe. But when next we find him, let us take him to one who will break this spell and reunite the family."

Rikku said, "It wearies me to think that all this strife began because of me!"

They did not speak again, and Jalla rose and walked into the darkness, gazing at the cattle. Rikku followed him, and they stood and talked about the cattle which he was to trek to Ligu's camp. Ligu's camp was in Kontago near the border country, some five days' trek from Malendo, where Jalla would be.

"This trek will prove you a man, my brother."

"By Allah's help."

Jalla said, "Belmuna is a good man, and so funny! He is a hunter with a stout heart, brave as the devil. You will enjoy him on the journey."

"When do we start?"

"At dawn."

Rikku went back and sat in front of the fire, listening to the sounds of the night. Gradually a stillness descended, and he dozed away among the ashes.

* *

They had been on the road now three nights and Rikku's feet were blistered. Belmuna was fresh as on the first day and even now he was crouching behind a rock, taking a steady aim at something Rikku could not see. He had his bow drawn taut and his muscles were tense and glistening.

Silently Rikku tiptoed close behind him, kneeling down

He looked down . . . and saw three men labouring up towards him (p. 60)

at exactly the same time as the arrow hummed away. Still he could see nothing with his untrained eyes.

"*Kai!*" exclaimed the hunter.

In one bound he leapt out of his hiding position and over the crest of the hill. Rikku stood up and peered after him. A thicket hid him from view, and when he reappeared a duiker was slung across his broad shoulders, a smile furrowed his face.

"Eating for this night," he smiled.

Rikku stroked the duiker. "You are a great hunter indeed. But, Belmuna, you brought news of the tax-gatherers. How now do you find time to kill for the pot when we should be fleeing."

"My little master, you know it is too late to leave this night." He put down his kill on a rock, and hastily wiping his hunting knife cut off the portions he required, leaving the entrails on the rock. "Good! We go now!"

Although they had been on the road for three nights they did not build their first resting camp till dusk. A light shower had begun to make its soaking felt. The shower developed into a steady downpour, accompanied by claps of thunder and a storm that threatened to root down the very walls of their shelter. Rikku and Belmuna, wrapped in straw rain-capes, went round the fences of the cattle, making sure they were safely ensconced for the night.

The rain pelted steadily down. The two of them crouched, one at either end of the enclosure, watching the cattle through the night.

Belmuna said, "In Allah's name, it will be a happy day when I hand over the cattle to their owner. *Kai!* A man to risk his life like this! Sleepless in the night, harassed in the daytime?"

To pass the time Rikku told Belmuna about Fatimeh and how Hodio had run away with her. He spoke also of his father's quest for the girl. "My father thinks I want Fatimeh. But I do not want her, really."

Belmuna laughed.

"My father! Allah spare his life!" Rikku said. "I shall be happy if we can set eyes on my father's face again."

"You think we shall ever cross his way? I tell you your father has vanished! Followed the winged creatures. Ha!" There was a pause and then Belmuna asked, "Tell me, Rikku, why did you ever choose to come with me?"

"Because my spirit agrees with your own. And again, you are strong and brave and full of adventure. You understand the hyena and the leopard. You are like an animal yourself."

Belmuna flung back his head and laughed, holding his sides. He ended his laughter with a little hiccup. "I am an animal, he, he, he! Hear that one! I am an animal. Oh, by Allah! You are a funny one!" His face suddenly mellowed. "Allah be praised."

They talked on into the night and it was Rikku who first shut his eyes and slept.

* * *

The sudden rumble of the thunder-storm woke him. He was dazzled by the big sweep of lightning that flashed over the veld, and for a moment, he saw the humps of the Zeebu cattle, their upwardly pointing horns.

"Allah be merciful," he murmured.

Dawn was a long way off, and this rain made him uneasy. He called out to the old hunter:

"Belmuna! Belmuna! Where are you?"

No one answered him. Instead he saw in the glow of a sudden flash two shapes crouching.

They were men. Momentarily the light fell on their dark faces, silhouetting them. Rikku's heart froze within him. He felt the evil in these thieves, the way they slithered forward under the rain, hissing, signalling fast to each other.

Lightning flashed again and Rikku saw them more clearly. They were severing the cords which held the cattle.

"Raiders!" shouted Rikku. "Cattle thieves!"

"Belmuna. Belmuna, where are you?"

He heard the patter of feet as the men fled. A sudden sinking feeling in the stomach darkened his spirit. Belmuna might have been surprised and killed. These raiders might have been at work long before he woke. He blamed himself for falling asleep: had he forgotten what the raiders did to his father's cattle?

"Rikku!" cried a voice from the gloom. "Come here. Hurry!" It was Belmuna.

Rikku seized his bow and arrows.

"Belmuna!"

And Belmuna answered: "*Na-am!* . . . I'm here!'

Rikku found that Belmuna had fallen into a thorn scrub. He tried to extricate him without hurting him.

"I—I think I got one of them; I'm not sure," the hunter

confided. "I chased him and shot him. We shall see in the morning. Ah, thank you. I'm free. Come. Come and see." He led the way. "This is where I cut them off. You were sleeping then. Here, by this stream. We should be able to recover the other cattle when the light comes."

"*Kai*, Belmuna. You are a man!"

"It is Allah that makes men," the hunter replied. "Some day when you're grown up like me, you'll be braver than I am. You'll fight for your rights and you'll defend your property. Come with me."

Rikku felt good. He followed Belmuna. In the darkness they could do little but wait. The rain poured down steadily.

* * *

They rested for two days. On the third day, in the grey of early dawn, Belmuna began to get the cattle on the move. He made clucking noises, his stick slung across both shoulders. There was a mighty rumbling of bodies thudding against bodies, of horns clashing. The cattle lumbered in a thousand opposing directions.

Rikku ran in front and around them, trying to mobilise them, cursing, using all the skill his father had given him. It was a nerve-racking affair. Rikku wanted to sit down and weep.

"*Tau!*" Belmuna exclaimed. "That is the way, boy! Soon we shall be away. That's the sun, it has risen and is up. Allah has awakened us all. Soon we shall be away."

He talked on in this encouraging manner until the herd

settled down to a good steady pace, except now and again when one of them strayed aside to pluck a juicy bit of grass or young leaves.

Rikku trailed behind, stopping now and again to lean on his stick. His eyes throbbed in his head. He yawned, and his entire body ached for lack of sleep. But the old hunter beside him was cool as ever, his wrinkled face shining, his eyes yellow and quizzical.

He was the first to see the men who were coming towards them from a great distance.

"Rikku, those are the tax-gatherers. They have caught us."

Rikku shaded his eyes against the morning sun. There were three men, and they looked like officials.

"Belmuna, what shall we do?"

Belmuna's eyes widened. "We shall play them a trick. *Wai!* They have caught us, but we shall play them a trick."

His whole body was tense. "You know, Rikku. I shall stampede the cattle. Ha! How can a man count stampeding cattle, eh? Ah! They have caught us, but they shall see!"

Rikku glanced nervously at the approaching men. Something about the two of them awakened a vague memory in him. "Belmuna!" He placed a hand over his mouth. "Belmuna, you recognise those two men?"

"By Allah, I do not know them."

"The thieves of the other night! They tried to rob us, and when they failed, they went to the tax-gatherers."

"The rats! Gently now, here they come. Smile at them. Be pleasant." He leaned a hand on Rikku. "I shall stampede the cattle. Listen. You know that ravine, the one near the rocks, the one we passed yesterday? We meet there."

Rikku's eyes fixed on the face of the official.

"Welcome!" He smiled. "Sannu!"

The official nodded. He looked tired. Rikku and the two traitors exchanged glances of hate.

"What's your name?" asked the tax official.

One of the thieves came forward eagerly. "He said your name!"

"My name?" Rikku turned that over.

"Your name!"

"R-i-k-k-u- S-sunsaye!" The official wrote that down. Without lifting his head, he said: "All these your cattle?"

"All this lot? Yes." He winked at Belmuna to stand by.

"Aren't you too young to own all this?"

"They are mine." Rikku glared at the thieves. "I did not steal them. When a man marries in our tribe, his father gives him cattle——"

"You are married?"

Rikku smiled. He must play for time. Out of the corner of his eye he saw Belmuna girding his loins tighter with the wet cloth.

"My wife is at the camp."

The thieves exchanged glances, while the official lifted his red fez cap and scratched his head. Rikku saw his lips moving. He was counting the cattle.

"How many?" he asked.

"You will have to count them. I cannot say exactly. Last night the thieves came. I do not know how many they stole." He talked directly at the two men who immediately busied themselves with the counting. "A man starts with twenty cattle, they have young and increase; or they have the rinderpest sickness, and they are wiped out. One gets confused."

"True," the official said. He folded his notebook and yelled at the men. "Get busy."

Rikku signalled to Belmuna. At the same time, he and Belmuna began to speak in gutteral tones. There was a strange wave of movement throughout the herd. The cattle began to get jittery.

"The time has come, Rikku."

The official strode forward. "Control them! Keep them together——"

"My Lord," said Rikku, smiling. "Don't panic so. Cattle are sensitive. They don't like strangers."

"Look out!" shouted one of the thieves as a big-horned bull charged him and knocked him down.

Rikku gave five taps on his stick, light taps seen only by Belmuna. It was the agreed signal. The cattle surged. They were now raging around.

The official sprang back as they stampeded past him into the veld. Swearing, with the wicked smile of vengeance, Rikku watched his herd, watched the gasp of dismay on the tax-collector's face as his precious calculation vanished with the wind.

"Till next time!" Rikku waved his stick, and away he darted, tearing down the hill in a direction opposite to that which the herd had taken.

Far out and away from them all, Rikku doubled back on his paces, ran fast along the dry bed of the stream, now and again pausing to make sure he was not being followed. He could see nothing of his pursuers. If they decided to follow the cattle, they would get nowhere. He had trained them to disperse in different directions, but to reassemble in one spot.

Close on mid-day he arrived at the agreed ravine. It was very hot with the sun directly overhead. Tsetse flies were buzzing about his ears. He crouched under a tree, watching the cattle return one by one, and counting them as they came.

In the early hours of the evening, Rikku milked one of the cows, and having drunk his fill, set out for the north country. He would have to march very hard, if he hoped to get safely to Ligu.

Belmuna would never show up. Unknown to Rikku, the old friendly hunter was dead. A few yards from the scene where the tax-gatherer had accosted Rikku two men lay dead. One of them was the thief. The other was Belmuna. Both had been gored to death.

CHAPTER TEN

Mai Sunsaye was sorry to leave New Chanka, but if he continued to stay there Hodio would never let him go. The air was fresh and sweet though slightly cold. He walked and walked, meeting nobody, not knowing where he was going in the rain.

Once he saw a hyena slinking across his path, and he knew the beast was returning late to its lair in the rocks after the night's havoc. Nature still slept. The rain stopped now, and the greyness in the east began to show flakes of red.

He began to meet people on the veld: mostly farmers, and a few bushmen with their sugar-cane-laden donkeys. Birds were beginning to twitter now in the trees. He saw a cuckoo, brown-winged and black-beaked, cooing away in the trees. He thought of Jalla, and he remembered that there was no one he would like to meet more. He thought of Rikku and wondered how far he had gone now on his way to the border country.

By the time he came to a stream, it was mid-day. He could see the marks in the grass where the stream had raged past, shortly after the rains. Already it was not more than ankle deep. Two or three donkeys were lolling in the sands while their owners washed their feet from kettles, preparatory to saying their mid-day prayer.

Mai Sunsaye joined them. He had not known these people before, but something about his manner made them ask him to lead them in prayer. A short while after they had said their prayers a man in tattered clothes came to him.

"You are travelling far?"

"I am looking for my son, Jalla."

"Jalla of the thousand cattle?"

"You know him, then?"

"Only a stranger will not know Jalla; he is always on the move. He comes, he goes with the seasons." The man in the tattered clothes thought hard. "*Wal-la-hi*, I cannot deceive you." He studied his chaplet carefully, counting the beads. "I hear he is moving southwards to the banks of the great river. You know, when they begin to burn the grass in this country, that is the time the herdsmen all move southwards. They are looking for green grass . . ."

"I have heard of that river," Sunsaye said.

When he had wiped the sand from his brow he set off, keeping to an old cattle track that ran in a network to the south. He was familiar with all the main tracks, and had once gone down to the great river in the south along one of them.

Day after day he journeyed. A week had passed when he stopped at a herdsman's camp on the way. He was a man who kept many dogs; middle-aged, with two children, a boy and a girl, he seemed to be blessed with many calves.

There were two fires always burning among his cattle, but still the flies came, even at night.

Mai Sunsaye remained with him for three days, and they talked about the great river.

"You spoke of the great river to the south," Sunsaye said. "Have you ever grazed cattle that way?"

"*Ai!* Where is it I'm coming from?"

"You did not tell me that."

"I was there twenty days. I made my camp under a baobab tree, the last big tree before you enter the village. The white men were digging for gold in that part of the river."

The little boy ran out of a hut and went among the cattle. He was patting their backs, and even pausing to de-tick some of them.

"My son is up early," his host said.

The boy ran across to them. "Mother says you should come and eat," he smiled.

"Me?" said the two men at the same time.

"You two."

"I have not finished my work," the cattleman said. "Sunsaye, you go first. I shall join you in one moment."

When Sunsaye got to the camp he found his host's wife sitting on a tiny stool, her wide shoulders trembling as she churned the milk, separating the butter. Mai Sunsaye could not help thinking of his wife Shaitu, and his daughter Leibe. Where would they be, now? So affected was he by his sudden sense of guilt that he stared hard at the woman's raven-black hair, seeing nothing.

"How now," she said uneasily.

"I am thinking."

"Of your wife?"

"*Wal-lah-hi*, of my mission."

The woman smiled and looked at him through the corners of her eyes, understanding him. She was indeed young, and a true wandering Fulani. Sturdy, yet supple, the lines of her body flowed like a stream over smooth rocks.

"You are thinking of your wife, and your children. You need them, and you want to go back. But this your son, Rikku, you love too much. And so you want to go on. Mai Sunsaye," she said suddenly, "why do you thus torture yourself? I am a woman. I know what love is between young and young. Fatimeh and Rikku. But now, has she not forgotten him? I swear she will not even recognise him, if she sees him. We live on the veld. A woman wants to work for somebody. Not wait. Fatimeh is not waiting."

Mai Sunsaye bowed his head while she talked. A smile hovered at the corners of his mouth.

"I for one, I believe that Fatimeh is alive. No, better still, I know it."

"But suppose she has married a very powerful man?"

"Let me find her first. Then I can show Rikku, and say, 'You see what I told you?' "

"By Allah, you do not act like one of us. I fear it must be something more than just your son's love for Fatimeh. It may be a charm, but who can tell? Something they put over you while you slept. Mai Sunsaye, there are bad people in the world."

The little boy brought a gourdful of rice and melted

butter. Mai Sunsaye took it from him. It was still warm. He sat on the floor near the woman.

"Something else? Do you also believe, like the others?"

She stopped working suddenly and looked at him, her eyes wide with surprise.

He said, "You want to tell me you have not heard. They say I am smitten with the *sokugo*, the wandering disease. Perhaps that is why I wander so, feeling restless all day."

She said nothing. Her eyes were downcast. Perhaps she was feeling sorry for him. He ate his rice slowly. Now he had done it, and must not stop here any longer. If she wouldn't talk of it with her husband, it would be a different thing. But he knew they would regard him from now on as an eccentric old man, and he did not want their pity.

All his thoughts were now directed towards the gold mines where he learnt Jalla was camped. He knew he was on the right trail, and at least it would take him less than seven days to get to the great river. His plan was to go from one village to the other, sometimes resting for a night where it was convenient, always asking questions and following the clues they gave him.

He ate little of the rice, and when he looked again at the woman to thank her, he found that her eyes were still downcast and her hands unsteady. Her husband soon joined them, smiling his approving smile at the large calabashes of sour milk which his wife had placed near the door of the hut. In a little while she would take them to the nearest town and sell them.

"I shall not sleep here another night," Sunsaye announced. He saw the woman begin to busy herself with moulding the cheese into balls.

His host said anxiously, "What is the quarrel?"

"None," said Sunsaye. "I have the wandering sickness. It has just struck again. I am like that. And when it strikes, I must either respond, or——"

"In Allah's name!"

"Or die!"

He felt a sudden giddiness and was afraid. Had he been exerting himself too much again? It soon passed away, and he looked up again at his host.

"Till we meet again." He extended his hand.

His host took his hand and held it. "May Allah bring us together."

"He is above, and He has the power."

Mai Sunsaye slung his bag over his shoulder, and went round to the back where the children were riding an improvised wooden horse. He stroked their heads with tender hands. Then with a determined set of his shoulders he strode down the old cattle trail, humming a tune.

At the corner, he stood and looked back. The cattleman and his wife stood together near one of the beehive huts. Their two children were gathered round them. He raised his hands and waved, and he could hear their cries and see their waving hands.

CHAPTER ELEVEN

Mai Sunsaye's first sight of the village on the great river did not excite him. He had been travelling through bush which thickened day after day, sleeping in trees, eating forest fruit, preaching at little villages on the way, and now the thought of seeing Jalla doubled his pleasure.

He followed the earth motor road. At intervals along the road he noticed little clearings lined with stones. Here a traveller might stop and wash his hands and feet in the water provided and say his prayers. When he arrived at the next one he washed his face, hands and feet in the water and said a short prayer before continuing his journey. The road wound on for another half a mile, and turning beyond a mahogany tree he saw the grass huts. There were about one hundred of them, all huddled together, and he thought:

"If ever a fire should break out here, only Allah from above can save anyone."

At the end of the settlement was a large mud house, roofed with pan, and near it stood a motor car. Mai Sunsaye wandered into the village, passing by the bell in the centre of the clearing. He was still wondering what had become of all the inhabitants when a great cheering caught his ear.

Travelling in the direction of the sound, he came upon a footpath where the grass had been trampled down, rather like a cattle track. In the distance he saw a crowd of men. It did not take him long to recognise the tournament in progress. It was the *sharro*, the test of young manhood. His blood thrilled as he remembered his own days in the ring. A Fulani youth who had not taken a flogging at the *sharro* would never find a maiden to marry him.

Of the two boys in the centre of the ring, one had a bundle of whip and was boasting. At first Sunsaye could not hear his voice above the sweet strains of the orchestra. He could see the players with their gourd horns, violins, calabash rattles which created a lilting rhythm. He was as thrilled as the contestants who had drunk the intoxicating concoction. Years flowed away from him, and his eyes shone with glee.

> "*Ai!* . . . Where shall we go
> To seek for Trouble?
> To the East shall we say,
> Or the sunset
> To Talata Mafara
> Or across the border
> The border where dwells Ligu,
> Ligu of the thousand cattle
> *Ai!* Like Maize is Ligu,

Better clothed than any
I am of Ligu's people,
I give darkness to my enemies
Yee-whoo! . . . Yee-whoo!"

The youth was trembling with intense excitement. His muscles stood in twisted knots, oiled and elastic. In complete contrast to him his challenger was cool as ice. He stood with feet astride, hands interlaced above his head, motionless. He did not even budge one inch when his opponent began to circle round him with a long whip, the leather-hide or *koboko*, looking for a tender spot on which to cut him. There was plenty of exposed skin above the waist, but from the waist down the challenger was heavily girded in leather cloth.

Suddenly the man with the whip made a feint as if he intended to strike. The onlookers drew in their breaths. But he merely withdrew and began his dance again.

The music hushed again as the whip began menacing the victim. The man who had his hands above the head had not moved except when he turned aside, in the face of the threat, to spit.

Then Sunsaye held his breath. In that brief interval he had seen the face. The man in the ring was Jalla, his son! Waves of heat rippled through his stomach. He dared not call out, for fear of destroying the boy's concentration. He dared not look when the whip descended. That blow hurt him more than it did Jalla.

But why Jalla in the ring? Who was his affianced? Surely Jalla was not going to marry without the knowledge of the family? When he looked up again, the eyes of the striker were bloodshot. His face seemed heavy with passion. It must have been that contemptuous spitting that had irritated him.

Sliding forward like a cobra about to strike, he brought down the whip with a resounding *thwack*! An answering sigh from the mob and a livid welt of flesh that rose on Jalla's body told his father that the blow had been dealt with a masterful hand and had gone home.

Mai Sunsaye clutched a stick and dared not breathe. How would Jalla take it? For a moment, there was intense silence.

Then with joy, Sunsaye heard the words:

"Dumaru, your blows are like those of a sick woman. Shame on you, Psaha!"

It was Jalla's triumphant voice spoken with the venom of contempt. Simultaneously the music began. The girls came out from the orchestras. These were elegant girls. They carried their heads erect, treading ever so lightly as if their steps would not compress the grass. Their arms were freshly oiled, their bosoms firm. Truly, Jalla could choose from any of them, and he would choose right.

They came up in single file, chanting Jalla's praises, stuffing kola nuts in his mouth to the rhythm of the music. The tallest of them nestled close to Jalla and whispered something in his ear. The crowd thrilled. Surely that must be the girl Jalla sought. She carried an ointment in a cup and this she began to smear over the face of the welt so that it shone in the waning light.

Jalla had not so much as moved. His challenger now selected another raw-hide whip and began testing it in his hand. The music became uncertain and soon it stopped. There was something sinister in the preparations the man with the whip was making. Some whispered that he was rubbing it with some poison: something that would irritate and circulate round the body in no time.

Just then the whip circled and was about to descend when Jalla let out a yell and broke through the ring. Men sprang back on either side, and watched him dash into the scrub. He did not turn round but ran with all his might, screaming. Nobody pursued him, and he ran on alone like one smitten with a sudden madness.

Sunsaye covered his face in shame. The crowd parted in small groups. The girls were wailing for they loved Jalla and wished him well. Only those who knew talked, and they talked low but not so low that Mai Sunsaye did not catch their words.

"He must have seen something," they said.

"Dumaru has given him the magic of darkness."

"*Tau!* Who knows? Were we in the ring with them? It is between them both and Allah."

"*Wal-lahi*, this is a great puzzle to me. I have seen the *sharro* in twenty years, but never a thing like this."

"I swear by Allah, it was the darkness magic."

"*Tau!*" shrugged a big man. "It is over. *Ai!* Why make a fuss about it. If a man comes to the *sharro*, he must have his own magic too. My heart is sad for Jalla, for he was brave, until the magic caught him."

Another man said, "He should have brought his own magic."

It was a disappointing end to the games. They all dis-

Just then the whip circled

persed, talking volubly. It was now sunset and soon the darkness would come. Sunsaye inquired about the way to Jalla's camp. The trail was barely visible in the waning light.

CHAPTER TWELVE

Mai Sunsaye approached Jalla who was seated, head bowed, before the hut. "My son!"

Jalla looked up bashfully. "Ah, father, you found me?"

"They told me of the camp by the great river where the white men mine gold."

"The camp is there." He pointed over the huts. "Shaitu, Leibe and I moved here after you left. Rikku went to the border with some cattle for Ligu. It is better for the cattle to be near good grass.

"True. Where is Shaitu?"

"My mother and sister are still in the village."

"By Allah! I rejoice." He rubbed his hands. "Reunion with the family at last!"

Jalla smiled. "Now you will feel more settled."

Mai Sunsaye drew a mat and sat down. "I saw a lot of people as I came. Has there been a festival?"

"They were coming from the *sharro*," Jalla told him.

"The *sharro*?" Sunsaye feigned surprise. "By Allah, was there a *sharro*? Had I known!"

Jalla raised his head. "Many thanks to Allah that you did

not see my disgrace. Father, when my opponent raised the whip for the third time, I saw nothing! Just a void! I was terrified, so I ran. Now, I am a coward and the girl I fancy will not marry me! A coward, you hear?"

Mai Sunsaye patted him on the shoulder. "One does not go to the *sharro* without adequate preparation. Next time I shall give you some charms against the *baduhu*, the giver of darkness. *Wai!* Are we not the makers of darkness? Have no fear. Next time, no one will frighten you. No Sunsaye was ever a coward."

"So I thought, but——"

"And so you are, all of you! Rikku, Hodio, and you, Jalla! Have not all my sons prospered?"

Jalla rose and smiled. He was looking more confident. "She's called Fiddiggo, my affianced. If you see her, she's tall, by Allah. And fair as an Arab princess. Sweet of voice, and gentle of manner."

Mai Sunsaye laughed. "If she's all you say, then she deserves your hand. Stop fretting. Give me a bowl of some food, and we shall plan for the next *sharro* meet."

Jalla turned, and Sunsaye saw the weal across his back. He sighed. "The first thing, Jalla! You must go and bury your *kobokos* in the grave of a former champion of *sharro*. Thus will his prowess pass in spirit to your own whips."

He watched Jalla kneading the flour, listening to him with half an ear. "There are other herbs and unguents which I shall show you. That will be later when I go with you to graze the cattle."

Jalla brought him the food. He ate in silence while Jalla

lit a large fire. When he had done, Jalla took away the gourd.

"Father, there will be a great play in the mining camp this night. The white man's bride has come from their country and they are giving her a welcome this night."

"Truly?"

"Yes," Jalla said. "And she's indeed pretty. I think I shall leave my cattle in the hands of my servants. It is my wish to go into that village——"

"And see Fiddiggo?"

Jalla smiled. "Perhaps."

When dusk fell Shaitu and Leibe walked into the camp. Sunsaye embraced his wife and spoke kindly to his daughter. They were overjoyed.

* * *

A huge camp-fire had been lit in the middle of the clearing a short distance away from the bell that usually assembled the labourers. As in the afternoon, the labourers were grouped around this bell in the form of a full moon. Molere and his European bride sat in chairs which looked like thrones. The yellow light blended and fused with the pinkish skin of the European girl. Her eyes were dark pools as they stared steadily into the heart of the fire.

The same Fulani girls of the afternoon with a few more were dancing in the space before the fire. The eyes of all the men were trained on Fiddiggo, but there were many more who were slender and of good skin and figure. The words of their song sent many a man's imagination in a whirl, and accompanied by the flashing teeth and the deft hip-swings of the maidens the effect was delightful.

As soon as the girls retired after their singing, the men followed them into the dark corners. Two or three men had already gathered round Fiddiggo but she spoke to Jalla.

"Ah, Jalla, my own!"

"Fiddiggo," he said tensely, gripping both her hands. "Fiddiggo you are mine. And I have enough cattle to make your father happy."

She laughed. "I do not want your cattle."

Jalla looked away, embarrassed. "Fiddiggo, by Allah. I want you. *Kai!* For you I took such a beating——"

"And fled from the *koboko*! In Allah's name, you are not fit to look a maiden in the eye."

"Every action has a reason."

"Your action had no reason, Jalla. It was the action of a cowardly man."

From the shadows, young men and young women were returning in pairs to the camp-fire, their hands linked. This was a lover's night and Jalla spoke passionately to his chosen girl.

They wandered off into the shadows and talked while from the distance they heard the music of the entertainers but did not mind. They sat on a log and talked far into the night, planning their future.

CHAPTER THIRTEEN

Dawn found Sunsaye unable to rise from his bed. His head ached and his body was heavy with pain. He breathed with difficulty. Shaitu gave him a concoction to drink and remained by his bed while Jalla and the boys took out the cattle to graze. In his dreams and in his waking conversation Mai Sunsaye talked ceaselessly of Rikku.

"I shall die, without seeing my son!"

"That you shall not," Shaitu assured him.

"He is even now on his way to the border country where Ligu lives."

"I have failed him," he moaned.

"Father, if it is about Fatimeh, you should take your mind off that woman," Leibe said.

Sunsaye raised himself on one elbow.

"I want to be moving on." His wife pressed him back. "Wait till Jalla is ready then we shall all move southward along the river banks. So get well soon."

Sunsaye rolled over so that he faced the wall.

* * *

In twenty days he had sweated away the pain and they were moving camp. The work involved would have frightened any stranger. But Jalla remained calm, concentrating his attention on less strenuous matters. While the huts were being pulled down and the pack-oxen loaded with the bamboo branches that formed their framework, Jalla called his father aside.

"We are forgetting something," he said.

"Truly?"

"By Allah, yes. Is a man to remain for ever single?"

"Ah, Jalla!"

"It is my wish that you go at once and see Fiddiggo's father. Do not be stingy over the bargaining. I am willing to give him twenty head of cattle if that is his price."

"I think three would be enough!" The old man waved his hands in Jalla's face. "You pay twenty head of cattle for a maiden because you are excited. Then when your head is cool, you begin to say 'If I had known!' "

"Go then, father. I leave it to you."

"I go," the old man said.

He took out a mirror and began to trim his beard. He worked on his face, smoothing and polishing till he looked like a young man. When he stepped out of the hut, there was something of the old spring in his step.

"*Kai!* Are you the groom? You look so fine!"

"Fiddiggo must know you have a fine father!"

He walked down the slope, Jalla following him all the way, and giving him a last moment's summary of the situation. As he spoke he counted his fingers.

"First, I shall have to go to market."

"What for?"

"Ah! To sell one of the bulls and use the money to buy some cloth."

"That is good," Sunsaye nodded. "You must also ask questions here and there, you follow?" He winked. "But be cautious how you set about it. Mind your enemies."

"Then we shall buy materials to build a hut for my wife."

"Good." Mai Sunsaye pushed him aside impatiently. "I go now before night catches me."

Jalla tapped him on the back. "Hah! How can night catch you when it is now only morning?"

* * *

Jalla walked back to the camp. He was pleased to see the progress they had made. The calabashes, milking utensils, mats, had all been neatly rolled up and loaded on to the heavy pack-oxen. The cattle were all lined up with one of the boys in front and two of them behind.

It was still too early to set out, and Jalla suggested having a little meal. Later in the afternoon he gave his word and like an angry river, the humps of the cattle started rolling southwards. Jalla stood aside, watching the magnificent sight that he had seen in a thousand moments of changing camp.

They moved slowly, and above their rumbling Jalla could hear the hoots and guffaws of the herdsmen. The six bulls which he had chosen stood tethered to a tree. Without further ado, he drove one of them to the Miner's Butcher, bought the choicest clothes they offered for sale, and returned, not much sooner than his father.

Mai Sunsaye did not smile; he refused to say a word until Jalla practically forced him to speak.

"That girl's father is a thief!" he declared.

Jalla leaned forward and peered at him, puzzled.

"He refused to take less than six head of your best."

Jalla smiled. "When you called him a thief, I thought he asked for twenty." He called aloud to one of his boys and said: "Here, you know the home of Fiddiggo's father, by the river?"

The boy looked blankly at the sky. "Lord, I——"

"Don't tell me you do not, or I shall kick your stomach open with my toes! Now, drive those six cows there. Tell Fiddiggo's father I send him my greetings. May Allah bless him."

"I hear."

Jalla turned to his father. "Have I forgotten anything?"

The old man was shaking his head ruefully. "The thief! What? Forgotten anything, after giving him six of your best?"

"Oh, yes!" Jalla smiled. "I nearly forgot the cloth! Tell Fiddiggo's father, I should have taken this cloth there myself, but we are moving camp. We are going southwards to the banks of the River Changuwa near Malendo. You hear that? Fiddiggo is to join us there." He handed over the parcel of cloth. "Give this to her."

Mai Sunsaye raised his hands. "I have seen some crazy marriages in my time, but this! No drumming, no dancing, not even a quiet bridal night!"

"Father, we are men of cattle. Our cattle come first, and since it is our wish to take them to better pastures, all else must succumb to that wish."

"Still," Mai Sunsaye maintained, shaking his head. "I wish Fiddiggo had received a big welcome. After all, she is so very nice."

They did not leave the neighbourhood of the mining village until the boy had returned. He was something of a half-wit, this boy. He gave one answer to a question this time, and the next minute he gave a different answer. Mai Sunsaye and his son became confused and started to wonder whether he had really done what he had been sent to do. Whatever he had done, there was nothing for it but to wait and see.

In the small hours of next morning, they set out after the main herd, catching them up just before mid-day when the boys had stopped to make a fire and to prepare a meal.

Jalla was amazed at the size of his cattle. They seemed to cover the entire grassland as far as he could see. Moving, their horns clashing, their jaws nibbling, they lumbered around the leather-clad boys who rested on their sticks, squinting as the smoke rose skywards.

"Sannu!" Jalla greeted.

"Sannu!" the herdsmen answered.

"All went well?"

"By the power of Allah, all went well."

"Praises are due to him."

Father and son sat down. They talked idly about the pastures they were going to visit. The boys hinted that they had met some cattlemen who knew the place and spoke well of it. Shaitu stood in front with the herding boys watching Leibe who was perched on the pack-ox.

"I shall build Fiddiggo such a hut!" Jalla burst out suddenly.

"We are talking of the health of your herd and you are talking of something else!"

"Let's be off!" Jalla said anxiously. "There is no time to lose."

Snatching short rests, forcing the cattle on at a pace too strenuous for them, pausing to help a cow in labour, it was not until the third day that Jalla and his men caught sight of the lush greenness that waited them.

They lost no time in unloading the pack-oxen and setting them free to graze. Jalla set about building his much-vaunted hut for Fiddiggo, and Sunsaye watched him, surprised at how independent his son had become.

Early the following morning a horseman cantered up and asked for kneaded flour and milk.

"I come from Fiddiggo's father," he said.

Jalla tethered his horse for him, while Mai Sunsaye took him into the hut. Custom demanded that Jalla be absent from home when she arrived. Jalla set about preparing a bed for Fiddiggo. He heard the cattle lowing outside and thought that very soon not the boys but Fiddiggo with her tender hands would be milking them. He heard peals of laughter coming from the hut where his father and the messenger were closeted, and knew that the conversation was going satisfactorily.

Suddenly, Jalla burst out singing. It was a tune that had been disturbing him since he woke. He had been hearing it in his head—sometimes soft and whispering, borne on the wings of the wind, but quite distinct. But now it haunted him, sweet and exhilarating, and he sang aloud and with happiness.

When it was nearing time for Fiddiggo to be brought, Jalla slipped away from the camp and wandered into the scrub.

When he returned he asked his mother about Mai Sunsaye, but she said they had not seen him.

"Did he not come after you?"

"He went after you," Leibe said.

But they could find no reason why he should go after Jalla. They waited but he never came back.

"The wandering disease," Jalla murmured and then he threw open the door of the hut and Fiddiggo, head bowed, was sitting within.

CHAPTER FOURTEEN

Sunsaye wandered over the scrub, heading southwards. He asked questions as he went. He spoke to herdsmen, hunters, travellers, men, women and children. He asked them about Ligu, and soon he began to bend his steps in the right direction.

Ligu, it appeared, was camped on the border country, near the town of Kontago. The last man he asked pointed with a crooked stick and said that if Sunsaye hurried he might still find her camped there. But he must remember this was the season when much movement took place in search of new pastures.

For days he wandered until at last he felt sure he had arrived within the area where Ligu might be. He saw two thatched huts, the mahogany tree, with the cattle tethered under it and he decided to seek help.

"It fits the description they gave me," he murmured.

"I shall go and ask them about Ligu. He who asks questions seldom goes astray."

Before he had walked a dozen paces, two hunting dogs

charged at him baring their teeth. They were high and well muscled, and their tempers frightened him.

He stood quite still like a man suddenly petrified.

A woman poked her head out of one of the huts. "What is it?"

"Hold your dogs," Sunsaye said, and when the woman had called them to her side, "I am looking for a woman called Ligu."

Her eyes narrowed with suspicion. "Ligu—of the thousand cattle?" The eyes searched Sunsaye closely.

"Just so. Ligu, the champion cattle grazer; of whom they sing at the *sharro* sport."

"Do not stand so far away." She spoke sharply, and the dogs with tails between their legs, slunk out of sight.

Timidly, Sunsaye approached. She was not a young woman. Her hands were large and strong, but she was fond of ornaments. Her ears, hair, and wrists were heavily decorated with expensive jewellery, and she wore a brightly coloured cloth.

"Who may you be?" she asked.

"I am many people," the herdsman answered. "Some know me as the great medicine-man of Dokan Toro, Mai Sunsaye, he who speaks like a bird. Some hold that as chief of Dokan Toro, I ruled well. Some again maintain that in my time I owned the finest head of cattle. Yes."

"Come in and sit!"

"If Allah wills," said Mai Sunsaye.

When he was seated within the hut, he asked the woman how far it was to Ligu's camp, but she told him to hold on; that one could not go to Ligu's camp without eating well.

She would not let him go until evening when the cattle came back, and a slim boy stood outside.

Mai Sunsaye waved and cried, "Rikku!"

Rikku peered into the room but saw nothing.

"It is your father, Mai Sunsaye! *Kai!* Allah's work."

He lifted the *zana* curtain and came out, spreading out his arms so that Rikku could run into them and be embraced.

"Father! What time did you come?"

"*Wai!* Rikku, I heard from Jalla that you were making for Ligu's camp!"

"Jalla?"

"Yes."

"I do not understand. When I got to his camp they said you were gone."

"No, Rikku; this was at the new camp in Malendo, on the banks of the River Changuwa where the white men dig for gold. You know that Jalla is moving the cattle south."

"Just so. We give our thanks to Allah."

Ligu glanced from one face to the other, grinning. She said, "Rikku, tell him about Belmuna and the tax-gatherers."

Rikku told how the thieves had come in the night and how in the morning they had gone to bring the tax-gatherers to assess the cattle. He told how he and Belmuna stampeded the herd and how Belmuna had been trampled in the stampede.

"*Wai!* Allah rest his soul. But on the day of death there is no doctor."

"So," said Rikku. His eyes were moist.

"I can see that you loved him."

Rikku began to sob, and Mai Sunsaye put his arm round

the boy. He had matured in the last few months. He had seen the horrors of life and known what they were. This was his age of development.

Ligu came towards Sunsaye, and curtseying begged him for forgiveness.

"When I saw you I guessed you were his father. He talks so much about you! He is such a good boy. I would do anything for him."

Ligu quickly prepared a meal and set the platters before them.

Sunsaye said, "Ligu, who told you that I like *paturi*? Rikku, did you tell Ligu anything else about me?"

They laughed, a little uneasily. Sunsaye leaned forward, grabbing his spoon with excited hands. He stirred the fresh milk well into the pounded and buttered millet. When he lifted a spoonful of the creamy paste to his lips, he rolled his eyes round and smiled.

" When last did I sit by the fire like this, eating food cooked by a woman?"

"You didn't want it," Ligu said.

"Did I not?"

"By Allah, you did not."

Sunsaye sighed. He ate his food slowly, staring steadfastly at the fire, his mind for the moment in dreamland.

"Rikku," he said, "the Bodejo of the cattle tax, did he catch you?"

"Father, the Bodejo did not catch me. We were betrayed. *Ai!* So we were. The Bodejo was a good man and true. Not for him the curiosity of the goat that leads him to salute the hyena."

"Lah!"

"I told you it was done by Ardo's men."

When he heard the name of Ardo, Mai Sunsaye frowned. "Ardo! Always Ardo!"

He finished his meal and they sat far into the night talking, while Ligu busied herself with household chores.

Mai Sunsaye looked at the humps of the cattle. He heard their clashing horns and watched their jaws grinding the cud. The firelight danced on the patterns of their hides. Browns, whites, blacks. He was happy in the company of cattle.

CHAPTER FIFTEEN

Mai Sunsaye sat for a long time, reading his Koran. Rikku had since gone to bed in his *lukuri*, a kind of rough bed improvised by the Fulani herdsmen. He heard Ligu in the background pottering around her chores. When all was silent, Mai Sunsaye looked up, and there was Ligu standing beside him, watching his meditation. She must have been there long before he became aware of her. Self-consciously he began to gather his scattered manuscripts.

"I have got word, but if you are too busy to hear me——"

"Ah, Ligu! One is never too busy."

"A word about Rikku."

"Rikku?" Mai Sunsaye's eyes narrowed.

"Yes," Ligu said. "I do not know—but by Allah if there is something worrying his mind, must we hide it?"

"What have you seen? Remember, he is only a boy."

"If I tell you what I've seen, you'd hardly believe. But I am a woman. My instinct aids my sight."

"Yes?"

"Some nights I hear him talking aloud; some nights, he

leaps out of bed shouting like one harassed by witches. Often too have I feared that he walks in his sleep, but what he is looking for I cannot tell. It is not usual for a lad to be wandering in the bush at night, is it?"

Mai Sunsaye smiled. "So?"

"Sometimes he doesn't eat for two nights. At other times, Rikku will just sit down. Graze the cattle, he will not. Talk to me, no. Are you sick? He'll not say! Mai Sunsaye, it makes me afraid."

"Ligu," Sunsaye said. "Allah be praised that you are not alone in your observations. You are a clever woman, surely. You see . . . I love the boy best of all my children. Jalla has prospered; Hodio, he is a brave one but weak in love; Rikku, he is the youngest of the males. They were five. Two died; can we blame Allah? He gives and he takes back."

"So," Ligu said.

"Now peace reigned in our house till the day we bought a slave girl named Fatimeh of the Kanuris. You hear me? You are a true Fulani of the pasturelands. Tell me, do you know that my sons fell to quarrelling over Fatimeh? Fatimeh loved Rikku, but Rikku was too young. You hear? Hodio wanted Fatimeh. He was strong and he took her and ran. And when she had left, Rikku pined, and so I came after her." He paused and said, "I hear now that Fatimeh ran away from Hodio. She ran to her owner Shehu, and then ran away from him. They say she is roaming the wilds with her own cattle."

"A woman to be avoided!" Ligu cried.

Mai Sunsaye sighed. "So you think. But in Allah's name one must try one's best first."

Ligu said, "I have heard of a woman in white who wanders in the bush with white cattle. They tell the story. Some say she is a ghost. There is no truth in the story. For how can a woman move cattle at night?"

"*Tau!*" said Sunsaye. "He who waits will see what's in the grass. I have been patient thus far."

* * *

Rikku was developing a new hobby, the trapping of birds. One day he went to examine his traps and he saw a strange-looking bird. Panic spread in the entire neighbourhood. Within the hour two hundred people were assembled round the trap, gazing at the golden-eyed bird that looked so dignified and beautiful.

At last a brave man from the crowd extracted it from the trap and announced that he had seen its like before. As he displayed it a man pointed and said, "I see a talisman on its foot."

They looked and it was not a talisman, but a piece of paper within a ring.

"*Wai!*" exclaimed Rikku.

"Take it to the Sarki (king)," they suggested. "Take it to him! By Allah, who knows what all this means?"

At this moment a little man forced his way through the crowd. "A white vulture!" he cried. "A white vulture! I have seen sixty festivals, and my grave is near. Yet never before have I seen a white vulture. O! by Allah, what does this mean?"

They were afraid of this man who was well known for his

prophecies, and did not want to give him a chance to deepen their fears.

"Bad luck!" he managed to say before strong hands tore him away.

Rikku kept the ring and next evening took it to the neighbouring town. It was agreed that he must not spend the night in the village, but must return the same night, however late the hour. If he did not see the white man who might be able to decipher the message, he was to leave the ring in the hands of the Sarki.

* * *

Evening had come now and Rikku had not returned. Ligu and Sunsaye sat in the camp. Whenever they saw anyone approaching they stood and peered.

The Bodejo and the tax-gatherers arrived in the camp. They were accompanied by the little prophet.

"Bad luck; he, he—eh!" he piped, disappearing before a vicious swipe struck him in the face.

It was indeed bad luck. The tax-gatherers assessed the cattle and Ligu was almost in tears when she thought how hard she had struggled to avoid these same men.

Still they saw no sign of Rikku.

CHAPTER SIXTEEN

Rikku was standing at a street corner in the city. A girl of about ten years approached him.

"You are wanted by a lady," she said, pointing at the minaret of a tall mud building.

"Me?"

"Yes. Follow me."

He hesitated. He had always been warned to beware of strangers in big cities.

She led him round the narrow space between two rows of houses, and nimbly climbed the steps. At the top, Rikku saw that he had been standing in a very conspicuous part of the town and that unknown to him the woman who was said to have sent for him must have been observing him for a long time.

"Go in!" said the little girl.

Rikku again hesitated.

"Are you standing outside?" said a sweet voice.

"Peace unto you," Rikku said, and went in.

The woman was seated on a pile of cushions. Behind her was a bed so high that two stools had been placed beside it.

The woman herself was beautiful in a dark way, and one glance showed that she was a Kanuri, of the same tribe as the beautiful slave girl Fatimeh. Might she then know something about Fatimeh?

"You are looking for someone?" she asked.

"I brought a ring, and a paper. We caught a bird and ——" He could not rally his thoughts. The woman had a hypnotic gaze that confused him.

"You are very young," she said. "You are indeed more handsome than I thought from a distance. I like you and I want you to live here."

"Me? Where did you know me?"

She smiled. "Is it not enough to see you at the corner of the street and like you?"

Rikku stared at her in confusion.

"But I was sent on an errand. My father is waiting for me. I must return to our camp this very night." Rikku saw now that she was dressed in Oriental fashion, with glittering bracelets on her slender wrists and something like a crown on her head. She stood up now, among her draperies and the smoke of incense was swirling all around her.

"I mean you no harm——"

"Allah above knows that. But you must not detain me. I am the son of a cattleman. We live in the pasture lands. For us the town life is not the life."

"So you do not like comfort?" She looked round at the exquisitely furnished room.

"I am used to discomfort. We live a simple life. The floor is our bed, and nature is always a companion. But above all, Allah drives the fly for the tail-less cow."

She smiled.

A maiden entered carrying a tray with glittering china on it and she offered Rikku a cup with dark contents. He felt like a man dreaming as he reached out and took the cup, staring, puzzled at the dark contents. He held the cup in his hands timidly, and said, "My father and I are looking for a girl called Fatimeh. She is a Kanuri, and a slave girl. Do you know her?"

"You say she is a Kanuri?"

"Yes, and she ran away from us. We have been searching for her since——"

A sudden spark came into her eyes.

"Listen to me, Rikku. By Allah, I like you. I want you to remain here and not go away, looking for that Kanuri girl."

Rikku said, "I do not understand."

She smiled. "You are too young to understand. Bend your ear to my words. My name is Kantuma. I have influence in this town. Not even the king would dare question all my actions. Stay here. I shall give your ring to whoever you intend to give it."

She shrugged her shoulders. "Remain here, and I shall despatch my riders to where they'll seek Fatimeh. They may find her, they may not."

She went out of the room, leaving Rikku to stare at the contents of the cup. He walked to the window and poured the contents down.

"Who? Who threw that on my head?" shouted someone from below, and Rikku rapidly withdrew.

Kantuma came back to tell him that the riders were gone.

She had sent twenty men on horseback into the woods to seek out Fatimeh. They would go from camp to camp, asking about her and they must return in three days.

"Let us occupy our time by playing cards," Kantuma said.

She taught him how to play cards. She also had an old Ludo set, and after Rikku had played with her for a while he forgot his mission and wished he had come to her all the time.

Once Kantuma excused herself and went out. Rikku heard her talking to a group of angry men, but when she came back, she told him it was nobody of consequence. When he was tired he bathed in scented water, and wore silk suits built for him.

In this manner two days passed.

* * *

Rikku was ill at ease. Finally he spoke to Kantuma.

"Why do you thus detain me?"

She answered him from her bath.

"Because you please me. You are beautiful to the eyes and your manner is gentle. Princes and Emirs would give anything to be in your place."

That was true. Rikku had seen the way she treated a young and dashing Prince who called to see her the night before. One had gone down on his knees, making overtures to her, but she had shut herself up in the room, telling him she was indisposed. He had left in a rage, while Kantuma laughed.

"I am not a prince," Rikku protested. "I know nothing about your city ways!"

He was afraid of himself. This was an artful woman, a sorceress, with a strange beauty. Sometimes he thought of her as a snake, coldly beautiful, but deadly when she struck.

"Rikku, will you be my escort in the coming horse race?"

"When will that be?"

"In two days' time."

Fresh from her bath and scented, she linked her hand in his. "We shall sit in the big pavilion and eat honeyed dates," she said. "I shall adorn you with all the finery fit for a young prince." Suddenly she said, "What is wrong, Rikku. Do you not like your life here?"

"I enjoy it, by Allah! But wait!" An idea had struck him. "I was thinking. Will you let me ride a horse at the races? I am a very good rider. By Allah, let me enter a horse!"

"All right! I'll give you my best horse. It's an Arab and it has plenty of wind and power. My brother used it in his fighting days."

A day before the races, a man came in with a message from the Bodejo. The Bodejo had read the paper attached to the vulture's leg. It said that the vulture was released in a place in South America about six months earlier. Would the finder please send full information about the date of capture, the locality, his name and address.

"Where is the value in that?" Kantuma asked.

"*Ai!* The white people are queer. Who knows?"

"Is that all?"

"That is all."

* * *

The race track extended from the foot of the hill where people were buried, to a foot-path which ran at right angles to it. The entire track was about half a mile long. The race itself was simple. Without any discrimination as to age, size or weight, one entered, lined up with the rest, and on the word "Go!", sped off.

Rikku watched them from his stall, and he felt that he could at least win a prize here. The crowd was thick, and he wondered whether his father was present.

When his race came round, Kantuma helped him take off his expensive silk gown, leaving the light jumper and the thick breeches.

"As soon as your race is over, Rikku, wheel round; I shall be waiting for you under that tree. Then we shall go home at once." She smiled a little anxiously.

He did not look at her face. He could hardly suppress his excitement. He tore himself away. Somewhere near the stables, a hand touched him. He looked round and saw Chikeh. The Forest Assistant was unshaven, and his eyes were wild.

"Rikku, where to?"

"To the races!"

"Have you seen Shehu?"

"Shehu?" Rikku asked in surprise. "No, is he here?"

Chikeh's manner, his abruptness, his wild eyes and impatient looks, caught Rikku's attention.

"No trouble, I hope?"

"No trouble," Chikeh said. "Only, he killed Amina my wife."

Rikku gasped. "The same Shehu?"

Chikeh did not answer but mingled with the crowd. Rikku could still not grasp the situation. He found the horse and mounted. He was determined to win that race, and then to ride home on Kantuma's horse.

He did win the race, but he knew that Kantuma would send riders to his father to recapture him.

* * *

He abandoned the horse on the outskirts of the town and sought shelter in a public drinking house. As he entered, he saw Chikeh seated beside the boiling pot of corn beer, his eyes red, a jug of the brown liquid gurgling between his hands. He did not seem to recognise Rikku. Amidst the harsh laughter, *gwogie* music and chatter, he was sitting alone with his thoughts.

Rikku slipped past Chikeh and the other people in the room. He looked for a suitable hiding-place, but something else caught his eye: the tall figure of a man rising from the far end of the room.

Hastily the man pulled the turban over his face but not before Rikku had seen his hard features. It was Shehu.

Rikku ran back into the drinking room, and called: "Chikeh! I've seen Shehu!"

Chikeh tossed aside his jug and leapt towards Rikku. "Where? Show him to me!"

Together they broke into the next room.

"They searched high and low. They tried the door and found it barred from the other side. At the end of the path a flight of steps rose to the top of the minaret.

Chikeh began to climb, and Rikku called out to him, "Be careful."

The steps trembled under Rikku's feet. He was terrified and did not want to become involved in this unexpected adventure.

Chikeh was calling out: "Shehu, open the door! Open the door if you're not a coward."

"Rikku went down into the courtyard and returned with a large club. He struck at the door three times and it caved in. The door did not lead to a room, but merely guarded a flight of steps.

Chikeh bounded up the stairs with Rikku close behind him.

The passage darkened. Rikku looked up and saw a large man barring their way.

"Where are you going?"

"We want Shehu!"

"He's not here; and do not go one step farther. This is no place for men."

"What?"

"It is the home of the veiled women."

"We beg your pardon."

Indeed Rikku had seen one or two faces, hooded and veiled, at the windows, peering curiously on. Somewhere among them must be Shehu, disguised. He could tell that.

"He's not in there," the burly man said severely. "And

let me tell you now. These women are the wives of the King's son. You'd better flee before he returns from the races. Ah! . . . Look!"

Down in the courtyard a young and elegant man was handing over the reins of his horse to a servant. He came quickly up the stairs, but stopped short on seeing Rikku and Chikeh.

"Who are you? What do you want?"

The burly man intervened. "I do not know them, my master. But I suspect——"

"They have come after my wives!"

"So I thought, but——"

"Call the men! Lock the trespassers up! What the——! Tomorrow they'll tell me——"

A number of armed men appeared. They seized Rikku and Chikeh and bore them down the steps to a dark room at the foot of the stairs. As they sat bemoaning their fate, a man's dark face peered through the bars into the room. Rikku recognised the face behind the veil. It was Shehu's and he was laughing and pulling at his beard.

CHAPTER SEVENTEEN

"You said you saw him at the races?"

"Yes," answered Sunsaye's men.

"When was that?"

"*Ai!* It is not a week since."

"What happened, then?"

"We saw him," one of the men stated.

"He ran one race and we waited; but his horse did not come back like the others."

Mai Sunsaye glanced at Ligu. It was early morning at the camp and they were standing in front of Sunsaye's hut.

"What happened the first day I sent you to the woman?"

"*Kai!* How did she not abuse us? She said she would tell the Sultan of that town that we were molesting her. So we left."

Sunsaye turned and faced Ligu. "What shall we do now? It is time to be moving the cattle southwards, but we cannot go without Rikku."

For the past three days all the other things had been stacked ready for moving. Ligu had told Sunsaye that there was no point in hiding up here in the border country. She had come here to escape the tax, but now she had been found and had paid a large sum.

Ligu cocked her head to one side, and listened.

"Mai Sunsaye, can you hear shouting?"

"A little." Sunsaye listened. "Yes, a little."

"It is the hunters," said the men. "They are burning the grass."

"*Kai!*" said Sunsaye, thrilled. "It is time to be moving."

In the distance they could see the tongues of fire. A blade of burnt grass, now all ashes, settled on Sunsaye's nose, and he brushed it aside. Birds filled the air, cackling and darting about in a panic. A hawk dived into the smoke.

"They are burning the grass," Ligu repeated. "It is time to be getting south, to the banks of the great river."

"And Rikku?" said the old man.

"After tomorrow, we move without him," Ligu declared.

* * *

Mai Sunsaye followed the bird. The woods thickened as he hurried. Soon the sun was up and the dew on the grass began to run streams. Whenever he came to the green-shaded watercourses, the music became louder, almost fairy-like.

On the evening of the fifth day, he came to a stream, and after washing his face and hands rinsed his mouth. The dullness in the sky depressed him.

He heard a crashing sound, and held his breath. The grass in front of him moved suspiciously. He saw a large shape rear out of the grass: a lion. Hanging from its mouth was a large monkey. The lion growled and leapt into the bush.

Mai Sunsaye shivered. He stood wondering whether to continue his journey for the rest of the day. He had begun to see signs of a village. He gathered his gown about him, and with terrified backward glances and frenzied leaps at the slightest rustle, he made the village before dark.

The first house he came to was that of a blacksmith. They had long since retired, and Sunsaye wandered about for a time before he crossed the anvil shed and salaamed at the door.

A grey-bearded man carrying a lantern high above his head opened the door.

"Who are you?"

"I am a wandering cattleman. I am going south. Can you give me shelter here?"

The blacksmith's muscular chest filled out with air and his face puckered scrutinisingly. "We have been having thieves here," he grumbled. "Are you a thief?"

Sunsaye laughed. "Mallam, I would not be asking you to shelter me, if I hadn't seen a lion today."

The man's eyes widened. "You saw that lion?"

"Yes."

"Did you see the—the others, too?"

The lamp was shaking in his hand. He drew Mai Sunsaye quickly through the door and bolted it.

Mai Sunsaye sat on the floor and took the kola nut which the blacksmith was offering him.

"My wife is preparing food for you," the blacksmith said.

In the meantime he expounded fully on the legend of the

lion. There was a woman, he said, who wandered about the savannah. Some people had seen her, and they said she always dressed in white. She came out chiefly at night, and some said she drove cattle.

Mai Sunsaye instantly suspected Fatimeh. "Is it a long time since she's been in these parts?" he asked.

"We began to hear talk of her, let me see, about two weeks ago."

Sunsaye sat forward. He held the blacksmith's rough hands with all the vigour of a fanatic. "That was when I came over this way. Tell me about the lion."

"That is what we do not know. The hunters who have gone after the beast say that wherever they see the lion's pug-marks, there they also see the cattle's. By Allah! It is puzzling. And never once have we seen a dead beast on the veld."

"It is not a man-eater, then?"

Again the blacksmith shrugged, replacing the rag on his shoulder with a big hand. "Have you heard of a lion that does not eat man?" And he laughed.

* * *

Mai Sunsaye could not sleep that night. He was first to get up at dawn, and was pacing the front of the hut.

The blacksmith came towards him and extended his hand for a shake. "How did you sleep?"

"Very well, Allah be praised!"

"How's the tiredness?"

"There's no tiredness, while there's life."

They hugged each other like brothers and exchanged greetings in this manner for another ten minutes, at the end of which the blacksmith offered him a kola nut. Conversation centred on the lion and the legendary cattlewoman.

"Let me tell you something," Mai Sunsaye said. "Do you know it was because of that woman I left my home?"

"*Wai-lah-hi?*"

"I swear!"

And he told him the story of the slave girl Fatimeh, his only encounter with her, how his son Rikku would never be happy without her, and how he had almost resolved to give up the chase.

But this new story gave him fresh courage.

"I was on my way southwards," he concluded. "But now I must wait and see. There might be something in your story."

Later that day, he called a barber to give him a haircut because his host told him he was looking like a heathen. The barber lathered his head, beginning the job of removing every vestige of hair on it, until it would shine like the egg of an ostrich. He had removed all the hair on the head, but was now holding Sunsaye's chin in a strangulating grip, forcing the air out of his throat. This was necessary to give him a clean shave. Sunsaye could not resist. He gasped for air. Circles of light danced before his eyes.

"And yesterday," the barber chattered lightly, "a number of horsemen rode past this place."

"So?"

"Yes," the barber said, wiping some lather expertly on his palm. He stropped the razor keenly on a leather band and glanced at the blacksmith who was working the bellows. "They were going north. Did they not cross you on the way?" "No," Sunsaye said. And then, "What town were they heading for?"

"Well, there is one woman in the north at a place called Kontago. Her name is Kantuma. She is the wife to a man called Shehu and he gives her orders."

Mai Sunsaye's breath stuck. He could find no words on his dry lips. "I am hearing you."

"That is all!" The barber stropped his razor. "Now those men, twenty of them, were riding to meet Shehu in this woman's home. So the story goes."

"Oh!" He could hardly trust himself to say more. "Shehu uses her house as a cover, is that so?"

The barber stropped the razor. "As the rumour goes, Kantuma has seized a little boy, and Shehu says he will not release the boy unless he fetches his father. The boy is a Fulani, so we hear. I only tell you this, because you are Fulani. And again I thought you met the horsemen on the road."

"Was one of them riding a white horse?"

"*Kai*, yes!"

Mai Sunsaye rose and swung his gown about him. "Blacksmith, I beg of you; can you lend me a horse?"

"By Allah's will."

"I am going back to Kontago."

"But why so soon?"

"The boy they have captured is my own son, Rikku; and, hear me well, there is already fire in that town."

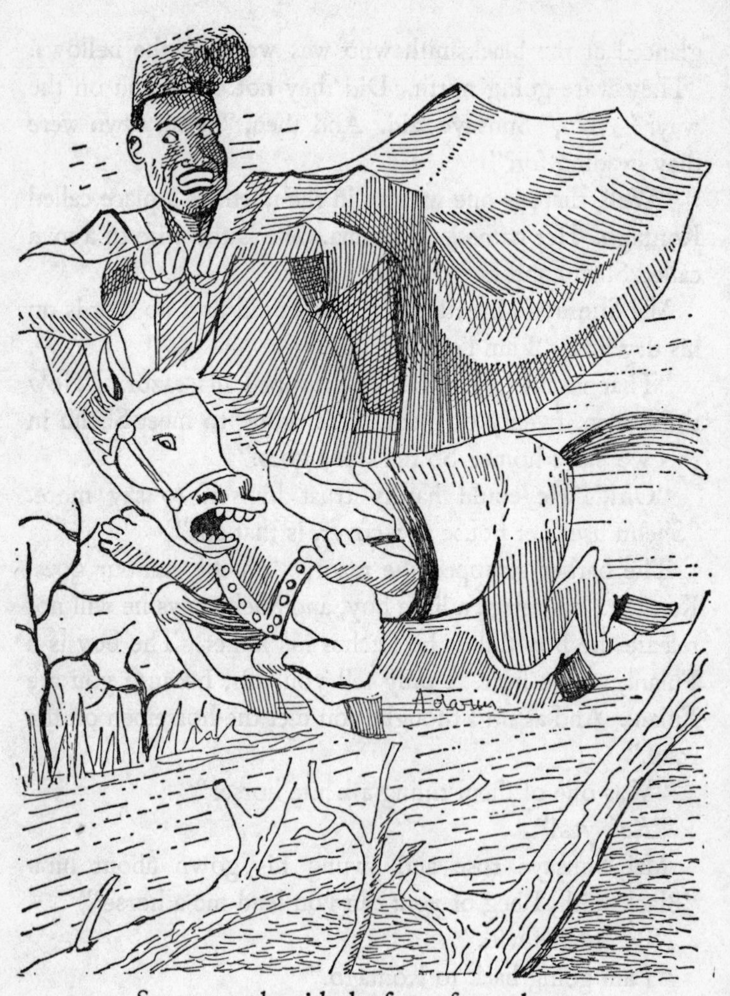

Sunsaye rode with the fury of a mad man

CHAPTER EIGHTEEN

Sunsaye rode with the fury of a mad man. His gown billowing out behind him, his eyes staring out of their sockets, he crouched on the wild horse beneath him, urging it on, ever onwards, while his legs dug into the flanks.

He passed rice fields, woodland, thorn thickets; he frightened gazelles, narrowly missed being gored to death by a buffalo; and still he rode on.

Towards dusk, he came to a stream where he stopped to water his horse. He had covered in one day what a man may walk in five. He bathed his hands and feet, and let the horse lap the cooling water. Suddenly he noticed that the horse was shy. He glanced round, sniffing the air, sweet and damp. Something was crying upstream and it sounded to him like the cry of a human child.

A short silence followed, and he drew the horse beside him and watched his tense ears. Just as Mai Sunsaye was about to remount and continue his journey, he heard the wailing sound again.

He went up the angle of the stream. There on the sands lay two children, so much alike, he knew they were twins.

He leaned over the children, murmuring: "Where's your mother, in Allah's name?"

From his robes he tore some cloth and used it to cover the naked bodies. As soon as his hands touched them, the forest shook with a resounding roar. He heard a crash through the woods. His horse shrieked wildly and broke away pursued by a lion. In one bound, both beasts disappeared up the stream.

He heard them struggle and when his horse shrieked wildly he knew what had happened. Now that his horse was dead, the lion would come rushing back at him. He looked about him for a means of escape. He saw none. On the opposite bank of the stream, a woman had appeared. She eyed him with amusement for a time, waded through the water, and with a nimble leap stood beside the children. Mai Sunsaye's mouth hung open in surprise. He could hardly believe what he was seeing: that this woman was the mother of the twins. She found a shady place and sat down with the children, suckling them. Sunsaye was shaking with fear.

"She's not afraid, the wild woman! She lives among animals. She is one of them!"

She smiled at him. There was something eager and young in her smile. She looked up for a moment and called out in a strange tongue. Sunsaye heard a thunderous crash in the woods. The lion had returned. It squatted beside the woman, licking its fangs, swishing its tail. The wild woman made tender noises in her throat.

She turned to Sunsaye. "Your horse is dead: what will you do now?"

Mai Sunsaye dared not move a muscle. His whole interest was focused on the lion which now regarded him with hungry eyes.

The wild woman said, "You must rest with us, what else?"

And with that she rose. Mai Sunsaye again observed how tall she was. Again she muttered something in that strange tongue and the lion bounded away. Then she turned to Sunsaye.

"The way is here," she said, in perfect Fulani.

There did not seem to be any way through the stream, but Sunsaye soon found that this girl knew more about the grassland than any cattleman. She moved swiftly through the gathering dusk, but by the time they arrived at her home it was dark. Her home consisted of one hut and one store. It seemed to Sunsaye that in a strong wind these flimsy structures would not survive. There was no clearing in front of the hut. From behind the hut cattle mooed.

"My cattle," the wild woman said.

"They're all white," Sunsaye observed.

"It is so."

"Then you are the strange cattlewoman of the legend! Allah have mercy on me."

"Allah forbid," the wild woman said. "I am not *korinrawa*. *Korinrawa* is a spirit. I am but a mortal. My name is Fatimeh!"

"Fatimeh!" Sunsaye cried, and threw himself into her arms. "Long lost Fatimeh! To see you and not to know you any more!" He stared at her unbelieving eyes. "You too do not remember your old father-in-law. But I have shaved my head. You do not remember Mai Sunsaye, father of Hodio, and Jalla, and Rikku? Lah!"

"My father!" shouted Fatimeh.

The lion appeared at the door. Fatimeh said "Do not be afraid!"

Mai Sunsaye would not say a word until she had ordered the beast out of sight. "Fatimeh, I have searched for you everywhere. I heard so many tales about you and your cattle . . . One night, I saw someone like you down south. I could not believe my eyes."

"Lah!" said Fatimeh. "Now Allah has united us."

* * *

All night long they sat up, Sunsaye making her recount her adventures. She told how Shehu had snatched her away from Hodio, and how in turn she had run away from Shehu and lived in the wilds. She met an old herdsman who had no child and she served him for a while. He taught her about roots and herbs and when they parted he gave her two cows and a bull—all of them white. She moved from one part of the savannah to the other: at night only.

About the lion, Fatimeh said that she caught it as a cub after killing the mother with a poisoned arrow. It was quite harmless, but a useful pet and it had saved her life many times.

Sunsaye listened, full of admiration. "The tales I heard about you! Some said you were a spirit!"

Fatimeh laughed.

Sunsaye looked at her twinkling eyes, the happiness and

cheer she radiated, and he was happy. His sacrifice had not been in vain. Now, at least he could take her back with him, and Rikku would never blame him again.

* * *

At dawn Mai Sunsaye saw clearly the wild state of Fatimeh's home. The grass around the hut was high and wet with dew and when it touched the skin it irritated. The hut was small and very frail, not furnished in the least. Fatimeh slept on a pile of grass.

"And you have lived like this all the time?"

"What do you see?"

"By Allah, I am indeed sorry."

She smiled. "You taught me to be a herdswoman. As a slave I had no right to love a free born man like Rikku. But now I have been cleansed, for I have brought forth."

"You have brought forth and by custom you are no longer a slave."

Mai Sunsaye remembered his mission.

"I must set out at once," he said. "Your lion has killed my horse, and perhaps is eating the flesh now."

"*Wai!*" said Fatimeh.

"I fear I may be too late," he wailed. "I'll surely be too late."

"Where are you going?"

"Kontago!"

"I'll show you a short way, then!"

"Now," said Sunsaye, "I must tell you the truth. It's

about Rikku. It has reached my ears that Rikku has been held captive by a powerful woman of the Kanuris. Her name is Kantuma and she lives at Kontago. That's why I am going there now."

Fatimeh's eyes flashed. "You are sure she has not abducted him?"

"I don't think so."

"I want to come to Kontago myself and meet this woman of my own people."

They were standing in a bamboo thicket as she spoke. Sunsaye looked at her and said, "She will not be more beautiful than you." A dove alighted on the bamboo shoots above their heads. Both of them watched it. The dove stood on a delicate branch, dangling its tail, trying to catch its balance. Something startled it, and off it sped.

The fever came then to Mai Sunsaye.

"Excuse me," he said, and followed the dove, the free dove, flying south.

* * *

Fatimeh had observed the bird too. She had seen Sunsaye's reaction to it. As he sped off, she rushed after him and seized him.

"What has happened?"

"Let me go!" Sunsaye cried, with a sudden swing of his arm; but Fatimeh's light grip was firm.

"Your eyes are all red, your tongue is out. Father, you have the wandering sickness."

"Lies! All lies!"

"So, that's it! You did not set out to find me; in truth, you have been following a curse——"

"Let go of my hand!"

He struggled and clawed. Fatimeh held him firmly and led him back to the rough shelter. She uttered a strange sound, and the lion appeared and mounted guard over the door.

"If you get up, he will kill you." She showed him the lion's pointed fangs and bare claws.

"I learnt a great deal about herbs from the old Fulani herdsman. Yes, otherwise I would be dead today. Once when I was very ill."

She began to mix some powders on a wooden slab, and presently she brought out some cold milk and stirred it in. The powders made the milk look green. All the while, she talked. Then she lifted the bowls and said: "Drink this: drink it, and whoever it is that made that medicine—that's right! From now on the *sokugo* departs from your body. Your body is rid for ever of the spirit."

She began to mutter words and soon she fell into a trance while Mai Sunsaye made a wry face at the taste of the mixture.

CHAPTER NINETEEN

Ligu had since given up Sunsaye and now devoted her energies to setting Rikku free. At Ligu's camp the boys were preparing to graze the cattle.

Ligu said, "I am going into Kontago," and she set off on her horse.

Near the mud building with the minarets she saw four horses standing ready saddled. Their reins were held by two little boys, each wearing a *kano* cloth and a small white cap. Ligu approached a man who was saying his prayers in a little clearing close by.

"Where is the house of Kantuma?"

The man looked up from his prayers with a shocked expression, as if to rebuke Ligu for mentioning so unholy a name to a man who was praying to Allah.

He pointed with his chaplet, and continued to count the beads. As Ligu entered, a man carrying a bale of velvet cloths and scents passed her.

"Is Kantuma there?" Ligu asked.

"She is up in the brewing hall."

Ligu passed a number of men in white robes playing

cards outside the door. Her heart thumped against her ribs in fear. She paused near the door and salaamed before lifting the matting which screened the room.

"Who is it?"

"It is I."

"Come in."

Kantuma was seated on a small stool, stirring a pot of boiling beer. Her eyes widened when she saw Ligu, a total stranger, within her kitchen.

"Is all in peace?"

"I have come to take my son away."

"Your son?"

"He has been here for more than one week now. We must go south. We do not want you to detain him any longer."

Kantuma's eyes fluttered. Ligu saw how beautiful she was and understood why she fascinated men. "He is not here," she said in a sweet voice. "I swear he is not here. By Allah, if you know where he is——"

"You cannot deceive me. You kidnapper of boys!"

Kantuma leapt to her feet, a tigress.

"Who's a kidnapper?"

"You took a young boy and tried to make him forget his father and mother. Understand this: we Fulanis do not like you town dwellers. We love our simple life which makes men free and brave and gives woman a strong position. Can you understand that?"

Kantuma glared at Ligu. "Get out of my house!"

"Are you serious?"

"Get out of my house!"

Ligu said, "Do not come near me."

But Kantuma had been foolish. She had raised the ladle and rushed at Ligu. Ligu who had been charged by bulls in her time, stepped deftly aside and as Kantuma struggled to regain her balance, she dealt her a blow on the back of the neck, rather as she had done to many a reluctant bull.

Kantuma fell, cursing. A black smear marked where a chair had bruised her face. A maid came in with a tray of china, but dropped it, screaming, and fled from the room.

"Wait and let me tell the Sultan about this," Kantuma threatened.

"You can tell whom you like," Ligu said. "Just as you can tell the king of this village, so also can I tell the king of all the herdsmen. Let me ask you, do you know whom you are talking to?" Ligu waited for a reply, but hearing none, she said: "Have you heard Ligu leave a task once she sets her hand to it?"

Kantuma's eyes clipped open. She said, "Ligu, champion cattle grazer, of whom they sing? I beg for mercy. Now what shall we do? I would not harm Rikku for anything. He is such a nice boy."

"I want him, that's all. The rains are stopping. The grass is drying. We must move southwards to the land of the great river where the grass is young and sweet."

"I'll tell you the real truth," Kantuma said. "We went to the races. Rikku rode a horse, and I have not seen him since."

"Where have you looked for him?"

A knock at the door made the two women turn.

"*Salaam!*"

"Who is it?"

But the man had already edged himself into the room. He was big and very black, and his dark whiskers swept across his face.

"Mallam Shehu!"

"My fine girl!" the big man replied. "You are striking some bargain with her?" And he indicated Ligu.

Ligu did not like his manners.

"Shehu," said Kantuma. "I'm glad you came."

"*Tau!* My pet. And you'll be even happier when I've given you this jewel."

He slipped a large glittering bracelet over her wrist and held it out for Ligu to admire. "Is it not nice?"

Ligu did not answer. Kantuma looked worried.

"Where did you get this?"

"*Ai!* Hinting that I stole it?"

"No, no. Only, I saw something like this not long ago. Was it not a prince who brought it here?"

Shehu's face darkened. For him the room seemed to have grown suddenly hotter. His face glistened with sweat.

Kantuma said, "This woman here is looking for her son, and she thinks I took him."

She told Shehu the story of Rikku and how Ligu had accused her of hiding him. Shehu's eyes narrowed.

"I must go back to my business at once," he said, and went down the steps without further preamble.

Kantuma and Ligu watched him through the window. He was directing his horse to the prince's house.

"He is a very bad man," Kantuma said. "Look where he is going."

"Do you think he knows about Rikku?"

Kantuma said, "It may be. Let us follow him at once."

She went indoors and produced two veils, handing one over to Ligu.

"Wear this," she said. Her manner had become brisk and very tense.

* * *

At the foot of the steps they mounted their horses. They rode through the alleys walled in on both sides, past the men leading donkeys to market, past the women dyeing cloth at the wells. The sun shone cheerfully on the guava trees, the date palms. In the middle of a large square, they stopped. They had seen Shehu wheel his horse into the Prince's compound.

"What shall we do?" Ligu asked.

"Follow me to the gate," Kantuma said. "I shall go in. I know the Prince. He often comes to my drinking house."

But before they had ridden a few paces, a dozen horsemen charged towards them. They came from the rear, in a torrent of hoofbeats and a swirl of dust fumes.

"We are lost," Kantuma said.

The horsemen stopped a few paces from them.

"Kantuma, long may you live!" shouted the foremost man. "We have just returned from our quest. They told us at the house that you had just left with a strange woman."

"Did you find Fatimeh?" Kantuma asked. "Did you see her on the veld?"

"We saw a woman in white, also cattle and a lion. But we lost the trail."

"We are on the trail of the enemy."

The men fell back. Kantuma and Ligu jogged onwards to the building that sheltered the Prince. Two orderlies met them at the gate and took their horses.

"Is the Prince at home?"

"He is in audience."

"Tell him Kantuma wants to see him."

The orderlies disappeared, and Kantuma and Ligu looked around the compound at the splendid horses that hung their heads out of the stable doors. Presently the man returned, and took Kantuma alone into the Prince's presence. Ligu waited outside, impatient.

CHAPTER TWENTY

Late that night, a weary Mai Sunsaye walked into the settlement where Ligu had camped. As he approached, the dogs began to bark, and a girl ran out shouting, "It is Sunsaye! He has returned." He saw that it was Fiddiggo, Jalla's wife.

"By Allah, Fiddiggo, you look well. Where is your husband, Jalla?"

"He's in the hut. He is not feeling well."

"Allah's blessing descend on him."

"The fever came on him of a sudden. But he took a medicine, and is improving. It was a long journey from Malendo. And now we have again packed all our things. We are merely waiting."

As she spoke, she was relieving him of his parcels, making a fuss about him, linking her hand in his, laughing. But beneath it he could sense her nervousness.

"Come inside, and greet Jalla. My mother-in-law, Shaitu, went with Ligu and Leibe to Kontago."

He went over to the hut where Jalla lay on a mat. Jalla's

face was drawn. Lines had appeared on his brow and his eyes were golden with a pale light.

"Jalla, how are you?"

"Allah descend upon us! It is high fever, but there is hope. The worst of it has passed."

"Allah be praised." He turned to Fiddiggo. "Let your eyes ever be on your husband's face. Let him want for nothing. Now Ligu, where is she?"

"I told you Ligu, Shaitu and Leibe, they have all gone to the town of Kontago. Ligu went first; then my mother-in-law was worried and went after her." Fiddiggo's voice was troubled. She said, "We are waiting to move south and we cannot move because Rikku is not with us."

"They've not found Rikku yet?"

"No. There was a fire in the town. All the grass houses were burnt down."

"By whose hand was that done?"

"We have not heard yet."

"I foresaw it! I foresaw it!" shouted Mai Sunsaye.

"Where are you going?" Fiddiggo asked. "You are not going to join in the fighting. It is too late! Wait till morning."

Mai Sunsaye laughed. "Fighting? What fighting? Then I must join in!"

"When they tried to get Rikku back and could not, Ligu hired some horsemen and they rode out to Kontago in force."

Sunsaye took off his robes quietly. He was growing more and more tense with excitement. He put on a leather jacket and drew his sword smoothly from the scabbard, then replaced it. The reassuring angle at which it hung from his waist made him smile. He belted two small daggers around his upper arm, and turned to Fiddiggo.

"There is still a horse?"

"In the backyard."

It was dark. As he swung deftly into the saddle, Fiddiggo hailed at him:

"Look for them near the mosque!"

* *

In the town of Kontago the streets were very dark. Sunsaye rode cautiously, peering ahead of him, watching out for Ligu's riders. Suddenly he found himself surrounded by horsemen who flung questions at him. It dawned on him that these men were laying seige to Kontago. At last, one man said:

"Welcome, welcome! We are Ligu's men."

"Thanks be to Allah. Now, how is it?"

"We are watching," said the leader. "It is tonight."

"Tonight?"

"Yes! We are watching. News has reached us that Shehu has planned to take Rikku and Chikeh away from Nigeria across the desert. We just heard it!"

"*Lah!*" exclaimed Sunsaye. "If I hadn't come!"

A hand touched Sunsaye on the shoulder. "Welcome!" It was Ligu.

"Ligu, forgive me for the way I left the camp."

"Allah forgives us all." She lowered her voice. "Your wife, Shaitu, and your daughter, Leibe. They are safe. Do not fear. I hid them in a friend's house. They should have stayed at the camp!"

Sunsaye said, "May Allah's blessing be with them! When the fighting is over, if I still live, I shall be so glad to see Leibe's face again!"

Ligu sneered. "You! The first thing you will do, will be to run after things that fly!"

"No, Ligu! That time has passed. I met Fatimeh; and she cured me of the *sokugo*. I shall wander no more, but return to my huts in Dokan Toro. That is my home. I am too old a cattleman to wander on the veld; like the young ones."

"You met Fatimeh!"

"In Allah's name, I did!"

"Then we must save Rikku."

* *

Ligu's men sat grimly on their horses. The night had gone far, and some of them began to nod with sleep. They arranged at once to sleep in turn, some of them keeping watch on the big house that belonged to the Prince.

Mai Sunsaye said, "If there's a back way, how shall we know?"

"There's no back way," Ligu told them.

It was then that Sunsaye saw the other cattlemen who were crouching at the foot of the wall. Still as ghosts they sat, with herding sticks in their hands. No one approaching would ever suspect their presence or that they had laid siege to the Prince's house.

It must have been soon after midnight when a hand

touched Sunsaye. He looked up and saw curious shapes engaged in mysterious movements in front of the Prince's house. He strained his eyes, and these shapes resolved themselves into camels.

From the house, a number of turbanned men came out. They carried no light. These turbanned men lifted two people and placed them on the camels.

"Rikku and Chikeh," whispered Ligu.

Sunsaye could hardly breathe. He crouched on his horse and saw the men in the dark turbans and long gowns mounting guard behind the two prisoners.

A whistle pierced the night. It was the agreed signal. All around the Prince's house there was a general stir. Then the foot of the wall seemed to come alive. Sunsaye and his men charged. From the dark building, armed men met their charge, shouting loudly.

The skirmish was short and bitter. Horses trampled on the limbs of fallen men. Camels neighed. The Arabs had drawn their knives and were using them in close combat mercilessly.

"Finish them off!" cried Sunsaye.

"Father! Father!" Sunsaye heard his son's voice rising eagerly out of the general din. His heart filled with joy. "Are you there, my men? Show them what you are!"

The cattlemen charged with redoubled vigour. Sunsaye tripped over a body, picked himself up. The body that had tripped him was Shehu's.

One of Ligu's men came to Sunsaye and told him that he had just seen Rikku disappear round the wall, supporting a woman.

Sunsaye ran there. He found his son taking leave of a wounded young woman.

Rikku was sobbing loudly. Mai Sunsaye stood by, not interfering.

"I die, but I loved you, Rikku, whatever I did!"

"Talk not of death, Kantuma——"

"Rikku, forgive! Your Kantuma dies. But you have Fatimeh. I see her now——"

"Kantuma!"

"You have your——"

Sunsaye saw her fall limp in his son's arms. He stepped forward then, but she was dead. He took his son away, saying nothing. But the boy was broken with sobs.

They did not arrive at the camp before morning, and there they found Ligu, Shaitu and Leibe, all waiting impatiently with Fiddiggo and Jalla that they might start the long journey southwards.

CHAPTER TWENTY-ONE

Indeed it was time to be moving the cattle southwards to the banks of the great river. Everywhere on the veld the hunters were burning the grass, throwing smouldering dung into the fields. At night the distant sky was illumined by enormous sheets of flame, and from the thatch huts in the village the people could hear the crackle of burning grass and smell the acrid smoke that choked the beasts and brought them running from their holes.

At night the brilliant glow threw shadows on the horns and humps of cattle behind the fences. Dogs barked and hunters crouched, waiting with arrows fixed to bows. They burnt the grass so that with the early rains the young sweet shoots of grass would push out and the cattle would graze with joy. It was their way and although the Forest Conservators had told them it was a bad thing for the trees, they would not stop when the season came round: a stealthy hand would always throw dry dung into the grass and vanish before the smoke exploded into flame.

As soon as Jalla felt some relief they all set out southwards towards the banks of the River Niger, in that stretch between Bussa and Lokoja where the waters are known as Kwarra.

When they had travelled southwards for three days they left Ligu to march on with her cattle. Jalla and Fiddiggo split away, travelling south-eastwards. At the same time Sunsaye and Rikku went in search of Fatimeh. They found the village of Dajin Bauma and there they inquired of a farmer who lived there where they could find a way to Fatimeh's camp. He showed them a cattle track which they followed to Fatimeh's camp.

Fatimeh was waiting for them. Ragged and unkempt, her eyes were wild and from her lips came a sad tale. The twins were dead, buried. She cried the whole night through and Mai Sunsaye gave her words of consolation, but she was still depressed. Between her and Rikku there seemed to be a new barrier which the old man could not yet understand. He had imagined that after seeking out Fatimeh and bringing Rikku to her the boy would rush into her arms, covering her with warm embraces. But it seemed to him that Rikku was regarding her with the eyes of a stranger.

In the morning, the old herdsman went down to the stream to wash his face and say his prayers before they set out to join the herd with Ligu, Shaitu and Leibe.

He heard a rustling behind him and turned round to see his son. "Father," Rikku said, "I have come to tell you something. It is something that has made my heart heavy since yesterday."

"Go on, my son. Speak now, or you will carry the burden even longer." He had already observed the tears in

Rikku's eyes. He turned away and poured water on his toes, rinsing them.

"It is about Fatimeh. I—I do not want her any more!"

"*Lah!* And after all the palaver!"

"Father, I cannot explain it."

"You fell in love with that woman in Kontago, and her death has saddened you."

"No, father!"

"When she lived, you saw her elegant manner of doing things, and the princes who courted her?"

"Not so, father."

The old man sighed. "Thus it is that our people are drifting more and more away from the hard life to the soft life of the city." He shook his head. "Even you, my son!"

"Father, all you say is not as it is. I want to wait a little before I take a wife. I love Fatimeh but only as a brother might do. I am only a boy now. In two more rainy seasons, I shall be ready."

The old man's head was bowed. He heard his son pleading with him, but all he did was go on rubbing his eyes in silence.

"I—I want to go away to New Chanka for a while to see Hodio," Rikku was saying. "Then I may return to Ligu and work for her till I am a man. That will be after two seasons of rain. Then, if Ligu is pleased with me, she will give me cattle and I can start on my own."

Mai Sunsaye saw his son very clearly now: a mere boy who had developed a strong calf-love for a woman older than he, a woman living in Kontago and more experienced in the ways of the world than he was.

"You speak well, my son. But first you will come with us to Dokan Toro. Your mother must know of this."

"Allah bless you, father."

Mai Sunsaye saw the delight in the boy's eyes, and he felt a sudden choking in his throat. He turned away so that Rikku might not see his clouded eyes.

"Go wait for me at the camp."

"Yes, father."

Rikku bounded up to the camp, a song on his lips. In the trees, the birds were singing too.

Mai Sunsaye returned to the camp to find a dejected Rikku. There was no sign of the lion or of Fatimeh. They waited and waited, and when the sun was too hot they began to move southwards and after two days hard trekking they caught up with the main group travelling to Dokan Toro.

Mai Sunsaye could never guess why Fatimeh had chosen to run away in that manner. Had she overheard their conversation at the riverside, or could it be that she too had sensed Rikku's new change towards her and could not remain with the family under the circumstance? Whatever it was, they never heard of Fatimeh and her lion any more.

* * *

At Dokan Toro they planned to remain with Sunsaye for a fortnight, so as to make ready for the great march southwards to the riverside pastures. The old man was home now. Home to him was the handful of huts outside Dokan Toro. To the Fulani herdsman who has spent most of his time on the move, home was a cluster of huts anywhere from which no more movement was contemplated. To Sunsaye the place was Dokan Toro.

There was much to delight the old herdsman now. He had found Rikku's Fatimeh, though the boy had since outgrown his calf-love of her. But more important to him, he had gathered the broken remnants of his family. He was certain that Hodio would do well as a dweller in the new town of Chanka. For Hodio, that would be a good thing and he would mature as a man; his wild streak would sober down under the routine of sugar manufacturing and building the new town.

Jalla was, of course, the old man's greatest pride. Jalla had shown what the herdsman's son can be. One thousand head of cattle, and Fiddiggo for a bride! But that defeat at the *sharro* must be turned into victory some day. The old man remembered his promise. As soon as he was a bit more settled he would prepare and send to Jalla a bundle of magic whips which he must use at the next *sharro* meet. True he could wish for no more beautiful bride than Fiddiggo, but the Sunsaye name must be retrieved.

At night when they gathered round the fire with Shaitu, and Leibe, and Rikku, each telling what they had seen and heard since they parted, the old man knew some of his former happiness. But he had lost his position among the people of Dokan Toro and to return to them now he must wrest from Ardo his chieftaincy.

He and his family had taken great care not to set up camp too near the village. One night Sunsaye and Rikku crept to the door of Ardo's hut. The dogs could not bark for their mouths were tied with magic meat. They woke Ardo up and confronted him with a choice between instant death and instant flight. In his scanty clothes, Ardo ran out of the village. He had not gone far when the flames began to burst out in each hut in turn.

In the morning Sunsaye and his supporters marched through the town. There was much feasting and rejoicing. Under the dorowa trees the maidens played the *gwogie* violin and rattled the calabashes while the young men engaged in gymnastics and feats of manhood. The flutes sang, the drums thudded, and anklets jingled on happy feet. To many this was the end of Ardo's tyrannical reign. They knew Sunsaye of old as a father and ruler. Willing hands soon cleared a site and set him up in good style.

For a while, Sunsaye felt he had once more taken up the threads of his old life. People came to him to have their fortunes told. They brought him their wounds of body and soul to heal. He was in his element.

In a short while, he knew Rikku would be going without him to join Ligu as herdsman. Rikku would work as apprentice to Ligu until she gave him some cattle to start off on his own. That was a good thing. The boy needed the sympathetic care of an elderly person. Let him go to New Chanka to see Hodio and his sugar mill. But to cattle he belonged and to Ligu he must return.

Early on the night of Rikku's departure, Sunsaye called him and told him he was feeling a queerness. By late night he was boiling hot and delirious. Now they saw that the old man had exhausted himself. He had under-estimated the strenuousness of his lone wanderings over the veld.

Rikku and Shaitu, with the aid of all the best herbs they knew, doctored him. It was to no avail.

"On the day of death, there is no medicine," Sunsaye told them, smiling.

It was the third day of his illness and they had battled bravely with death.

"Rikku!" His voice had become a faint rattle. In that brief instant when the smile broadened on his lips, he breathed his last.

Rikku answered him, running. But alas, he was too late. He began to cry and to throw himself down in grief, and Shaitu held him, crying too.

Sunsaye was indeed well beloved and they buried him in great pomp on the spot where his first camp had been. Then they cleared away in great haste. For legend holds that the place where a man has died is bad luck.